REALMS OF THE
GOBLIN KING

LISA MANIFOLD

GOBLIN POP PRESS

Realms of the Goblin King © 2017 Lisa Manifold

––––––––

Want more of the Realm? Sign up for my Newsletter or Follow Me on Amazon!

 Created with Vellum

To my darling boys.
You show me the stars are within reach.

1

Brennan

*I*t was dark. He blinked, and the darkness didn't change. Iris! Where was Iris? They'd been lying in bed together when he noticed a red light beyond the window. He blinked several more times, wanting to see if he was still in his room. He wasn't. And—whatever it was he was laying on, it wasn't his bed. It felt—he felt like he was in a cart or wagon or something like it. Iris wasn't there. He felt the slash of fear for her.

Where was he? Where was Iris? Who had done this?

His mind leaped to the answer before he'd even finished the thought.

Cian. It had to be Cian. Who else would be interested in harming him?

He moved his arms and legs, to see if he was hurt. Everything still moved, although it was apparent he was bound in some manner. He closed his eyes again and listened. He sent out a spell, meaning to break his bonds.

Nothing happened. Brennan tried the spell once more and felt a sting as the spell hit his skin.

He was bound not only physically, but magically as well. Being tied down and unable to use his magic left him off-kilter. He felt as though he hovered on the edge of the castle wall, about to topple over. Breathing deeply, he focused on making the rest of his senses alert, aware. He hadn't been in a battle for a long time, but he was now. The situation was nothing less than a fight for his life. A fight for everything he held dear. He could not forget that. He found that he shifted into battle mode quickly, as though it were an old cloak. To escape, he would need to be able to see the opportunity.

There were others around him. He could hear the movement of one—two people. No one spoke.

While nothing covered his eyes, he couldn't see. He took a guess that since he was magically bound that his eyesight was restricted as well. This was powerful magic--he would need to remember that also.

Where could they have taken him so quickly? Was Iris harmed? He focused on her, wanting to see if he could sense her, or was close enough to her that she could sense him. He concentrated hard. She wasn't near him, but she wasn't able to hear his call, either. He rubbed his hands against his legs. He was clothed, and it felt like his clothes, at least. His hand caught a shape in one of the side pockets of the pants. Was it possible? He must have left it in a pocket—how had he gotten dressed? Another question to which there was no answer.

He sighed. Even if he did have it, he wouldn't be able to manage it in this situation. He would need to hide it as well.

Brennan pictured the castle and his family. He could try to call them mentally. Unfortunately, he could not manage that sort of thing with Iris. Yet. Another thing for her to learn, once he got out of this. The thought of her in danger was a knife in the gut. Let her be safe.

If he was honest with himself, she hadn't been safe since he'd met her. The argument could be made that he'd increased her chances of having an accident or worse since the moment they'd met--he'd practically landed on her in a human bathroom. Once he and Drake, who'd been with him, had righted themselves from their fall, Drake had sent them back to the Goblin

Realm with Iris in tow. Drake had initially thought she was a spy of some sort.

Now she was his love and his wife. And she was alone.

Brennan pulled his thoughts from Iris. She was strong. He would need to trust that not only was she strong enough, but that his family would protect her.

Who could he reach? He and Drake often communicated this way. He sent out a plea, a shout of his brother's name.

Faintly, he heard, Bren?

I'm alive! I've been taken; I'm tied—

A blow hit him in the head.

Iris

We were in Brennan's study. Ever since we'd found the note, stabbed into Brennan's shield, with a message of *Come and get him*, I'd been living in the study. As had Drake, Jharak, and Taranath at various times. It was starting to show the signs of people camping out. I would need to get one of the cleaning staff in here, open some windows. Fear and worry had a smell, and I could sense it all throughout the room. Pungent, stinky, kind of like old shoes. Yeah, we needed to air this place out.

Drake was pacing, thinking out loud as to where Cian might take Brennan. He stopped in the middle of what he was saying, an odd look on his face. "Bren?" He asked softly.

Then he started, and ran to towards the window, clutching at the sill as he leaned out to the glass.

"What is it?" I asked, following him.

"I heard him! He can't be too far, or I couldn't hear him!" He pushed off from the window and turned, heading for the door. "He might still be within a close enough distance to find him!" He stopped at the door of the study, hand stilled. I could see the concentration on his face, and his brows pulled together.

"What?" I asked.

"I can't hear him anymore!" The anger and frustration made him sound fierce.

"Try again!" I urged.

He glared, and closed his eyes, taking a deep breath.

The atmosphere of the study was thick as I waited to hear something, see something from him. Anything to get a clue as to where my husband was. I was frightened. How had they—whoever they were—gotten inside the castle? Inside our room? I'd seen the red light out the window, and the next thing I remember is waking up alone.

His shoulders sagged, and he let out an explosive breath. "Wherever he is, he's not there now."

"What does that mean?" I asked, trying not to explode. This was so frustrating! And wholly inadequate. I thought a king would have amazing systems in place to...to what? To find people when they're lost? Something. I didn't know what, exactly. Everything else seemed to run so smoothly here. But I was frustrated with the lack of it. Whatever it was.

"If we're close enough to one another, we can communicate—" Drake began.

"Yeah, yeah, I know, all telepathically. I know! I don't need a lesson. I want to understand why you lost him!" I had my hands on my hips.

"Because if I had to guess, he's not conscious," Drake ground out. "Your Majesty."

I backed away from his anger a few steps, bumping into one of the chairs. Grabbing onto it like a life raft, I sank into it. "What do you mean? Is he..." I faltered, not able to say the words.

"I don't know," Drake said, and the anger had gone. He sat across from me. "He told me he was tied, and he'd been taken. I guess he meant tied or bound. Then, the thought just...stopped."

I could feel the misery from the pair of us permeate the room like another bad smell. Apparently, misery was up there with fear and worry in the stench department. I wish I didn't know this. I knew he wasn't angry at me, but neither of us had anyone else to snipe at.

Jharak and Drake had come running in when I screamed as I realized that Brennan was gone. The small crowd of fae that had attended our wedding were still there. Somehow, Jharak had gotten the guests on their way, claiming that Brennan and I were tired. How he'd managed that when we'd planned for a week-long party, I didn't know. At the moment, I didn't care. We could think up something later. When we got Brennan back.

Drake briefly told me about it—apparently, Jharak did the wink and nod thing, hinting that we couldn't get out of bed. Had Brennan not been taken, that wouldn't have been very far off the mark. One more reason to hate on Cian. So much for my honeymoon!

Jharak then had the unenviable job of telling Nerida, Brennan and Drake's—and Cian's—mom what happened. She had not reacted well. She hadn't been at the wedding, choosing to stay at their home in the Fae Castle, which sort of sucked. She'd ordered Jharak out before the wedding when they'd discovered that their son, Cian, was not dead as previously thought. She and Jharak were still on the outs, and an excuse for her absence had been made. I'd heard a few remarks from the guests as asides, but I'd ignored them. She wasn't my mom, and I refused to take her on as my problem.

Looking at my father-in-law, I thought he looked tired. In need of a long nap. I'd always seen Jharak as calm. Not now. He was not doing well, although I wouldn't have known if I didn't know him a little.

I wanted to feel more for him, but it was hard when I got stuck in wanting to smack the shit out of him. How could he have raised such a monster as Cian? I knew that wasn't fair, but it was how I felt. At least I could acknowledge I was unfair. Baby steps, right? I knew he was just a place for my anger and fear to land. Maybe it was more Nerida's fault.

So no snark Jharak's way. I got the impression that Nerida's continuing anger had shocked him. Drake told me that everyone was surprised when she chose not to attend our wedding, her husband most of all. Drake said that Jharak had tried to call her via mirror before the ceremony yesterday. I didn't get the sense it had been a pleasant call. She hadn't shown up, although I knew he'd planned to ask her again, now that things had changed drastically. You know, now that the Goblin King was missing. Maybe get her to be helpful like families were supposed to be in times of crisis. Hopefully one of the helpful bits was to be a damn parent to your kid. The non-psycho one.

In my opinion, she hadn't been much of a parent,

and more of a hindrance and a pain in the ass ever since Cian popped up like a bad case of the flu. I didn't count on much from her, but I understood that Jharak, Drake, and Brennan had a relationship with her and loved her.

I'd be polite if she decided to grace us with her presence once more. "I might as well go get dressed. You think Nerida will show up here?" The thought of seeing her as angry as everyone said she was made me a bit nervous.

Drake gave me a rueful look. "I don't think it will matter what you're wearing, but it's probably a good idea. As for Mother, I don't know. She's angry with the three of us, and since you married Brennan, and aren't on Team Cian, you'll be lumped in with that."

I felt my anger rise again. "Oh, she's cool with one brother continuously trying to off the other one? Not even counting me, because you know, human and blah, blah, blah." Maybe I should leave for a bit if she did show. Nerida wasn't the only one who was angry.

"We could set Mara on her." He raised an eyebrow.

I stared for a moment and then burst into laughter. I'd seen my grandmother and Nerida butt heads. Mara had decided to support me with Brennan, but let Nerida put her kid above me, and I think Mara would open up the proverbial can of old lady whoop ass. Not that I'd call either of them old to their faces. I wouldn't live long enough to get the words out. The thought made me laugh harder. Mara had been unimpressed that Nerida wasn't there for the wedding. Nerida would be behind before she ever got started.

"I don't know who would win that one," I gasped weakly, leaning forward with laughter. Mara had gone home with my parents after the wedding celebration had started to get a little wild. That, and she didn't want my parents to get sick. Humans didn't do well in the Goblin Realm, or anywhere else in the Fae Realm. My parents didn't look bad, but there was no reason to push it. Mara didn't know about this.

"I agree," Drake said, rising. "They both are good at feeling relatively righteous about their cause, even though I don't know Mara all that well."

I waved a hand. "No, you're on track with her. I wouldn't take her on. Where are you going?"

"I am going to see my father, to see if we need to prepare for my mother coming here. That will give you the time to get dressed, and present yourself as you should be." He bowed his head a little, and then with a smile, left the room.

Drake didn't hint well. I lifted a hand to run it through my hair, and I could feel snarls in the back. No, that wouldn't work at all with my brand new mother-in-law. Who hadn't been to the wedding by her choice, but I had a sneaking suspicion that wouldn't matter. Not if she rode in on her high horse. Since Drake and I would be leaving shortly—I wondered if I'd mentioned that to him—to seek out her son, kill his ass, and rescue my husband, I felt pretty sure that more drama and mess were headed my way.

I sighed, and stood up, heading back to my chambers. I'd always heard that clothing gave you confidence. So it was probably a good idea to get myself together and look like a Goblin Queen should.

———

*a*n hour later, Drake came back into Brennan's study. We both went there as a matter of course. It was Brennan's favorite room, and I think it made us both feel better to be in it. He had not only Jharak but Taranath with him as well. Taranath, the court mage, was one of my favorite people here in the Goblin Realm. Just knowing he was here, on our side, made me a little less worried. Not by much, though. I felt that I existed in a quiet state of terror. What if he wasn't—

No! I stopped myself. I wouldn't think it. He was alive, although probably hurt. But he was alive, and we'd get him back.

No Nerida, I noticed. I was glad I'd dressed

appropriately and equally happy that Nerida hadn't arrived.

Nevertheless, I needed to be supportive. Act diplomatic. "How did talking with Nerida go?" I asked Jharak.

He sat down, looking guilty. "I didn't contact her directly but wrote her instead. I don't have the patience to deal with anything other than getting Brennan back. It's one of the things you learn the longer you are together. Some things are better communicated via letter."

I shot a quick look at Drake, and he shrugged. Apparently, this wasn't a well-known fact in the family.

"Well, she can't ignore this, even if she's all about Cian right now," I said.

Jharak lifted his shoulders in a shrug. He looked tired. "I don't know what she will do, Iris."

I waved a hand. I didn't want to dwell on what Nerida might do because it made me feel sort of sad to see Jharak like this. "We'll handle it if and when she arrives. What I want to talk about is what we're going to do next. We need to go look for him."

"I'm not sure that's a good idea—" Jharak began.

"What would be a better idea?" Drake interrupted. "Wait for whatever it is Cian is planning next? Sit here, like helpless children? No, Father, that is not the best idea. We must seek him out."

I nodded. "I want to go."

"No," two voices began. Maybe three.

Drake crossed his arms, saying nothing.

I stood, giving them all the evil eye. "My husband has been kidnapped. If you think I'll sit and wait for others to get him, you're insane. I'm going." I looked around, making eye contact with each of them.

"I don't know how much help you'll be," Drake said.

"I think you may not be strong enough for what we face," Taranath added.

I turned away, taking a few deep breaths. This was the right thing to do. I knew it. I could feel it. I loved him more than anyone—well, in a different way. I couldn't negate how Drake felt about him. Or Jharak. I had to handle this. I was the Queen. That meant I got to say what happened. They'd fight me on it, but I needed to be strong. Be more than the Iris they thought I was.

When I faced them again, I made my face calm and told myself *don't yell. Whatever you do, don't yell.* "Jharak, I will need to ask you if you are willing to stay here and manage the Realm. I know that you are away from your Realm, but I think Nerida can handle the Fae Realm, even if she's unhappy with you. Will you do that for Brennan?" I'd almost said for me, but Brennan was his son.

Jharak looked caught between the proverbial rock and hard place. He glanced at Drake, and then back at me with a half-grin. "Well done, Iris. Or should I say, your Majesty? You managed that nicely. I really can't say no, can I?"

I shook my head, allowing a smile to break on my face. Not a big one, because I didn't want to gloat. "No. You can't. But there's no one else outside of Drake I trust to take care of Brennan's—our—Realm. Since Drake is coming with me, it has to be you."

"You're not coming with us," Drake said.

"Oh, but I am. You're not leaving without me."

We both gave each other the stink eye. I know he was all bad ass, and in a bad mood, but so was I.

"Brennan will have my head," he said.

"Brennan can't do anything right now," I shot back. "We have to get him away. Did you tell them what you heard?"

"What?" Taranath and Jharak asked together.

Drake told them how he'd heard Brennan speak to him, that he said he was tied, and that Drake lost contact with Brennan when he tried to respond.

Taranath began to walk back and forth, fingers steepled and tapping one another. We all watched him until after a moment he stopped. "I don't think he's dead," he said finally.

Okay, really? I'd just gotten my head away from those thoughts. Jharak didn't look thrilled, either.

"Why not?" Drake asked.

"Let us look at this logically. Cian wants to hurt Brennan. That is something that has been obvious in every interaction Cian has initiated. He's angry, and he wants to inflict harm. Quickly killing Brennan would not inflict enough damage on Brennan himself. It would hurt us, those who care for him, but it would end any suffering he has in store for Brennan. So I think it fair, unless we hear from Cian directly, to assume that Brennan is alive. He is probably hurt, but I would say he is alive."

"Okay, then what?" I asked. Impatient as I felt, it made me feel better to hear someone other than me say Brennan was alive. The fear that he would die that they would kill him before we could find him—that fear sat at the back of my mind, always there, always waiting to remind me. It showed up when I woke alone and hadn't gone away since. I had shoved it as far back as I could, but it was there. Taranath's words calmed me, a little. I'd take even a little at this point.

"We need to decide where Cian would hide Brennan."

"The Dragon Realm," I said immediately.

Jharak held up a finger. "Ah, no. That would be the last place he would go."

"Why?" I demanded.

"Because he knows we are at..." he stopped.

"War with the Dragon Realm," Drake finished.

Jharak glared at his son. "I don't wish to use those words. Words have power, Drake. Words give life to things that might otherwise die a quiet death."

"Stealing our king isn't an act of war?"

"It would be, had the representatives of the Dragon Realm done it," Jharak said. "As it is, they can deny Cian, and state they know nothing about him, and they are involved in a dispute with our realms based on our calling off the engagement."

"Plausible deniability," I said. "Sneaky."

"We are not dealing with half-wits," Jharak said. "You must remember that always. The spell on you was only the beginning. And even that—it's not evidence of war. It was poorly done for Ailla to bespell you. But some will see it as Ailla attempting to remove a rival. They have planned this well. So we need to be careful. If asked, I shall say that we are at odds with the Dragon Realm, and the Goblin King is working to resolve it. I will not mention his being missing."

"You're going to go along with her crazy ideas, Father?" Drake exclaimed. "You know she's not up for this!" Furious, he threw a hand in my direction.

As though there was any doubt of who *she* was. I crossed my arms in front of me and glared at Drake.

Some brother-in-law he was. So what if Ailla had put a spell on me before? She wouldn't be able to manage that now. Not with Taranath around. Regardless of anything else, I'd pit his talent against her any day.

"Love is a powerful motivation, and we don't know what Iris is up for, do we?" Jharak asked.

Wow, he was good. "You think I will be okay?" I asked.

"I don't know," he said, turning that intense gaze of his onto me. The two different colored eyes always caught me, made me look twice at him. "But you will be accompanied by the fiercest warrior I've ever known, and one of the best mages in any of the Realms. You are as strong in your motivation as they are, and Taranath tells me you are coming along well in your lessons. I predict he'll keep them up as you travel. One thing I have learned, Iris, is that one cannot predict what will happen under stress. Sometimes, skill comes when least expected." He looked away for a moment.

It made me wonder what he was thinking. But then he looked at me again.

"I will expect, as the Goblin Queen, and the only ruler of one of my Realms that I consider to be in safe hands, you will not endanger yourself needlessly. I must insist that you will take the council of those with you. While it may seem overly cautious, they are both very skilled, and for me to agree to your proposal, you must agree to my terms. I do not want to see you harmed."

His eyes turned frosty.

I inhaled, looking for a way out. He'd boxed me into a corner pretty neatly. Drake was smirking. Yeah. Right. I wanted to listen to Drake. Jharak's words hit a sore spot. I was it for the Goblin Realm at the moment. And if we didn't find Brennan—I would really be it.

But we would find him.

"All right," I sighed. "I agree. But you two must promise to be honest with me. Don't hold back information because you think I might not like it, or cry, or whatever. You owe me that."

"As their Queen, indeed they do." Jharak's voice was firm.

Now it was my turn to smirk. Drake opened his mouth to protest, probably, but the look on his father's face made him close it again. I could see why Jharak was so good at being the king. He made it difficult to say no.

"Are we all in agreement?" Jharak asked.

"Yes," Drake muttered, rolling his eyes.

"Yes," I said. The fact that Drake was annoyed softened my irritation.

"Of course, Your Majesty," Taranath bowed his head. "I will serve my Realm as needed."

"Good," Jharak stood. "Then I shall go and see about readying horses and provisions for you. I suggest you pack. Maybe your mother has responded," He said to Drake as he made for the door.

I hadn't seen this side of Jharak in some time. He'd been so unhappy with what had happened with Cian, even before Brennan had been taken. It was as though a part of him disappeared for a while. It appeared, however, that the Fae King was back.

While it meant that I would have to put up with Captain Annoying, I was willing. If it meant seeing Jharak more himself--I'd put up with Drake, and more. I watched him leave with my heart feeling lighter than it had since I'd woken up and discovered Brennan gone.

"Okay," I said to my two reluctant traveling companions. "What do I bring for this trip?"

2

Iris

I stood, maybe an hour later, in the middle of my rooms. I'd gone through my closet, but there didn't seem to be much in the way of practical clothing. I could see my beautiful wedding gown peeking out of the wardrobe door, and my heart fell.

When would we get him back? Would we get him back? I could feel my resolve fall straight to the floor, and I sank into it. Tears streaked down my face, unbidden, at the thought that something might happen that kept me from him.

No. No. I couldn't think like this. I had to think positive. We would get Brennan back, and between the three of us, we would kick Cian's ass. Ailla's too if I could manage it. I'd probably need help but...I didn't care. I was so angry she'd put a spell on me that nearly imploded my life. Well, all the relationships that made my life worthwhile. She needed to go.

The door burst open, making me jump.

"Are you packed?" Drake asked.

I got up, wiping the tears. I didn't want him to see me crying or to give him any reason to try and boot me from the rescue mission, but I couldn't hide them, either.

"I don't know what to bring. None of this clothing is right for traveling or sleeping on the ground, or whatever it is we have to do!" I had visions of something like The Hobbit in my head as far as what this journey would be like.

Drake stopped. Clearly, this was out of his realm of expertise. "Show me your clothing."

I pointed, and he strode to the wardrobe. He looked through it and pulled out two dresses.

"Only two outfits? I'm going to be gross!"

"You think I am bringing fresh clothes for every meal? Really? These will be good because they are of sturdier cloth versus everything else you have." He held them out to me, bunched in his hands.

I stood, hands on hips. "Two? There's got to be something more."

We frowned at one another, in a standoff. Then he tossed the bundle of clothing at me, and said, "What do you suggest, my lady?"

I caught it. Hearing Drake speak to me in the same manner he did to Brennan made me feel better. Weird, but better.

"I have an idea, but I need your help. And thank you," I said.

"For what?"

"For coming to find me and making me stop sitting here feeling sorry for myself."

"Sorry is not going to get you any closer to Brennan," he said, but the irritation had faded from his tone.

"Yeah, yeah, I know, but it makes me feel a little better just to cry,"

He rolled his eyes and walked closer to me. "What's your idea?"

"I need to go back to my parents' house."

"No. Absolutely not. Traveling to other Realms is not like skipping across the room!"

"Which is why I need your help. I want to make sure I do this as efficiently as possible. I haven't portal traveled on my own yet, and I don't want to screw it up."

"What is it you feel you need from there?"

"Jeans, sweaters, a hat. Regular shoes. Clothes that

don't flow," I snapped, gesturing towards the wardrobe. "How do you fae get anything done?"

"I manage just fine," he snapped right back.

"That's because you're a guy, not hampered by a skirt."

"You're not some random human girl any longer, Iris. You're the Goblin Queen, and you need to—"

"I'll be the widowed Queen if we don't find the King. This will make things easier for me. Can you just work with me, rather than argue?" I lost patience, tossing my hands in the air.

He didn't reply, just stared at me for a moment. Then he smiled. "Change isn't always a bad thing. I suppose the Realms will survive the Goblin Queen being odd."

"Thanks so much for the vote of confidence. So will you help me or what? Please?"

He muttered in Fae--probably so that I couldn't understand him, but I got the gist of it. He stood next to me, and then looked down.

"What are you going to tell your parents? They won't be happy about this," he warned.

"I don't know! I haven't thought that far ahead yet, but I'll manage."

I closed my eyes as he pulled one of the magic-enhancing stones from a pouch—did these guys always carry them? It was something I'd been wanting to ask and kept forgetting. I might need to start carrying my own magic rock purse.

Then the walking through water, rippling effect, and we were in my parents' living room.

They were in the kitchen, and both looked up and froze when they saw us.

"Iris!" Mom recovered first. "What are you doing here? Aren't you on your honeymoon?"

"What is Drake doing with you?" Dad got to the more salient point.

"I need to grab some of my clothes," I said, making a break for my room. It had only been a day. They wouldn't have boxed up all my stuff yet.

"Wait!" Dad called, and I could hear him coming after me. "What's going on, Iris?"

I ignored him, going to my closet to grab a bag. What would be best? Three pairs of jeans? That should keep me. And underwear. I needed a fair amount of under—

"What is going on?" My dad repeated from the doorway. "Where's Brennan?"

"Brennan is not here at the moment. He didn't want me to come back to grab clothes. But I'm finding it easier to train in my own clothes," I lied, focusing on my dresser.

Silence. I looked up. He had the, yeah right look on

his face, one eyebrow up, and his arms crossed. "Trouble in paradise?" He asked.

I burst into laughter, surprised that it came so easily. Trouble in paradise summed things up nicely. "No, Dad, there's no trouble! Merely a…" I hesitated, looking for the right way to phrase it. "A disagreement. That's all. I promised to train in private, but I get to train dressed how I want." I finished stuffing clothing into my bag and headed for the hall.

"Why the rush to train at all? And why is this a fight?" He let me pass but followed me, right on my heels.

"Because we have a difference of opinion. It's one of those things you have to work out, you know, as a couple?" I put irritation into my voice, hoping that this would calm them, and throw them off.

We'd come back into the living room, and Mom heard my last comment. She and Dad looked at one another not even trying to hide their smiles.

"Looks like you and Brennan are well matched," Mom said.

"They are," Drake cut in. "And I will be on the unfavorable list for helping Iris, but I believe one is the best judge of how they will learn. We had better return, however, Iris, before we are missed." He looked down at me, and I couldn't believe what a good liar he was. Not a hint of the strain of the morning showed on his face.

"Probably a good idea," I smiled, struggling for the same calm. "I'll be back in a while to see you all," I told my parents.

Mom came over to me and gave me a hug. "I love you, sweetheart. Good luck."

"Good luck to you, too," Dad said to Drake, and he smiled.

Maybe we'd get away with this farce.

"I thank you, but I've been on the other end of disagreement with Brennan before. This is not the first time, nor will it be the last. But thank you for the good wishes," Drake said. "Iris, are you ready?"

I nodded, unable to speak. The reality of this—lying to my parents, the fact that I was about to go racing off through the Realms, having no idea where Brennan was, if he was even still alive—hit me right then. I hoped Drake would get us out of here fast. I didn't know how much longer I could keep this up.

He did something, I didn't see what, and the ripples started up again. Brennan had been right. This would get easier. I looked at my parents as we began to fade, and I saw them exchange a look. Oh, hell. Maybe we didn't pull it off.

I couldn't think about that now—the thought of Brennan made me want to cry and kill all at the same time. I straightened my shoulders and did my best to stand tall as Drake brought us through the portal. We were safely back in the study, and no one waited for us. Which meant that he'd done this well.

"You have to show me how you do that," I said. "It's nice not to feel like I'm going to throw up every time."

Drake frowned. "Has portal travel always been that way for you?"

I shook my head, letting the bag slide off my shoulder. "No, only since..." I stopped, thinking.

"Since what?" Drake asked.

When had I begun to notice it? When I went back with Brennan, meaning to tell my parents I was staying...that was the first time. It had been bad, like almost-puking bad.

"When Brennan and I went back together, and I ended up staying there." I sat down in one of the chairs. "Why did it start then?"

Drake sat across from me. "That may have been when Ailla cast her spell. Immediately after that, we discovered his note in the castle. Maybe she got in here as well? I don't know, Iris! It makes me irritable not to know."

I nodded, thinking about it more. "That makes sense, even if I don't have any proof. I hadn't felt that bad before when we traveled, and I haven't since."

He looked angry. I felt the pang of guilt I always felt

with Drake on the subject of Ailla. It had to suck to carry the guilt of loving the woman your brother was supposed to marry. Even if she had been putting on an act. I felt sorry for him, even though I knew my pity would piss him off.

"She is so much craftier than we ever gave her credit for," he said. "I am annoyed I was taken in by it." He gazed away from me, lost in his thoughts for the moment.

The pang of guilt grew. I couldn't keep this up. I knew he'd talked to Brennan, but he and I needed to have it out—I realized, with a flash of insight, this was more for me than him, and that made me feel like a jerk.

I still needed to talk to him about this. And—a thought came to me. I'd be honest with him. Completely honest, and tell him why I needed to say whatever I said. Even though this was for me, I needed to have the air cleared. Because Ailla would die. Not only for what she did to me by casting a spell on me and nearly ruining my life. Her involvement with Cian now sealed her fate, as far as I was concerned.

"I can't imagine finding out someone you cared for was not who you thought she was," I began carefully.

He made a noise that sounded like he was disgusted. "I am irritated with myself on many levels. I am normally more astute than I have behaved, and I am worried that I have put the Realm at risk."

"How do you feel about it?"

Drake gave me a look that could have frozen water. "How do I feel? It doesn't matter how I feel, Iris. It—"

I held up a hand. "It does matter. It matters to me. I know you're all I can get past this and whatever, but people, even you, have feelings. I feel sorry every time I mention her because I keep imagining how I would feel in your shoes. To me, whatever I'd feel is pretty shitty. And I feel for you. So I'm asking, as hopefully your friend, how you feel?"

He opened his mouth, closed it, and then leaned back in his chair. He looked tired and more worn than I'd seen him since Brennan was attacked before we were married.

"I feel like a traitor. I had no business feeling for her at all," he said stiffly.

Okay, so he wasn't comfortable with this conversation. Neither was I. It needed to be said, however, and we'd both have to awkward talk our way through it.

"Well, things happen. It's not the end of the world. You didn't act on it or do anything that would hurt Brennan or the Realm. So I think you should ease up on yourself. I'm actually inquiring for more selfish reasons."

He immediately looked happier at the thought of talking about me. "How so?" He asked.

"I want to know that you're okay when I talk with you about how to..." I stopped. Saying the words was different than thinking them.

"Kill her?" he asked.

I nodded. It sounded like a good idea in my head, but speaking the words aloud...that didn't feel great.

"It hurts. I won't lie. I don't like the idea. And then I tell myself that the Ailla I knew is not real at all, and merely someone manufactured to gain a result." The lines in his face hardened.

"There was probably some of who she really is, but...I hate to admit it, Drake. I think she's an awful person, and no one here knew her at all. The fact that she cares for Cian, even after knowing what he has planned, and this other stuff with the dragons...that's not what decent people do. I wish I could help you to stop feeling bad." I felt like a little kid, wanting the teacher's approval, but I did feel for him, and I didn't want this to hang over our working together like a funky smell. I might be young, but having fought with my parents and lived in small spaces while I did so taught me that things had to be brought out in the open.

He looked at me, and I couldn't read the expression on his face.

"Do you think that? Honestly feel that way? That she could have shown some of her real self, and still be the wretched traitor to all fae as she has shown herself to be?"

I nodded again. "You're a very black and white person, but most people aren't."

"What do you mean, black and white?"

"It's either one way or the other for you. There is no middle ground. I am starting to see that you and Brennan have lived that way for a long time, but it's not just the two of you against the world anymore, and the world is a hell of a lot of shades of middle ground."

To my surprise, he laughed. "I talked with Brennan about Ailla, and he told me you called him a candy ass. Is that right?"

"Yes, it's true! He was totally being a coward about talking to you. I understand because I didn't want to have this conversation now. You and I, we're not as close as you and Brennan, and we're going to have to be in close quarters soon. I didn't want to feel like crap every time we talked about how to deal with Ailla."

"You mean you're not testing my loyalties?" A skeptical brow raised in my direction.

"No! Why would I do that?" I meant it. "Your loyalty has never been in doubt, even though I have some hate at how many times you've hurt me." I grinned to ease any sting of my words. "I know you're loyal. So does

Brennan. But it's human—" I stopped. He wasn't human.

"We're not human anymore," he said softly.

"Does that mean you don't have feelings? From everything I've seen, the fae are just as big of drama queens as humans are! They hide it in some sense of superiority, but they are no better! Brennan is still mad at your parents. Your mom is falling off the deep end. Cian is holding a five-hundred-year-old grudge, and Ailla is one big ball of hate and anger!" I felt my fists clench.

Drake laughed again. "You're right. We're just as emotional as you humans. But we manage it so much better, and may look down from our lofty height in safety."

"Hey, whatever you have to tell yourself to make it through the day," I rolled my eyes. "Not how it looks from here, but whatever. I just want to make sure you're okay with us talking about possible outcomes for Ailla." I still couldn't say it.

Drake leaned in, his hands clasped in front of him, all laughter gone. "You have to say it, Iris. You could end up being the one to do it. There's no guarantee of who kills whom here. If you cannot say it, you won't be able to do it."

"Can you?" I challenged.

"Absolutely. If it comes to it, I will kill Cian, and

Ailla, and even Eilor. They are a threat not only to my king and queen but the lives of all in the Realms. Not just here, or the Dragon Realm." He gave me the eye.

I sighed. "If it comes to it, I will kill Cian, or Ailla, or Eilor. Because you're right, they are a threat to all the Realms. I don't like it, though."

He leaned back, shrugging. "No one does. Please don't believe that my acceptance of what we will need to do is any indication of me liking or condoning it. But it is what we have to do. We are tasked, you and Brennan and I, with defending the Goblin Realm. Brennan and you as his Queen have greater responsibilities. The Dragon Realm and Cian have threatened all of those." He sighed. "I'll do my best not to put you into that situation, Iris. Killing is different than we think it is before we must do it. I'd spare you that for as long as possible."

"Do you have to kill others often?" I asked, not sure if I wanted the answer.

"Brennan and I had to do so on the day we met you. But often? No. Brennan prefers to rule with diplomacy and negotiation." His mouth twisted. "I don't always agree, but this is why Brennan is a king and I am not."

"Do you want to be? Why haven't you been in line for the Fae Realm? You're a son of Jharak."

He laughed. "I'm human-born. Jharak would name

me in a moment if the other Realms accepted it. I am a member of the royal family, and always will be, Mother notwithstanding. But the ruler of the Fae Realm must be fae. It's all right," he said, seeing the look on my face. "I don't want to be a king. I prefer direct action and no prancing around with words. I'm content where I am."

"So we're all good?" I asked.

"We were never not good," he answered.

"Well, I feel better."

"And since it is all about you, your ladyship, I am delighted to be of service."

Hearing him tease me as he did with Brennan made me warm. I felt like this would be my home, even if was not yet so.

Drake stood. "Now that we've sorted your clothing, and your feelings, is it possible to find Taranath and decide on our next move? Or is there something else your ladyship needs?"

I stood, laughing. "No, long-suffering courtier. You have been of perfect service, and all my girly concerns have been addressed. Lead on."

The door burst open, and Jharak burst in. "Nerida has heard from Cian."

3

Brennan

*H*e opened his eyes slowly, feeling how scratchy it felt to do so. He'd lost track of how long he'd been here. His arms and legs were still bound. He closed his eyes quickly as he heard someone enter the room. Wherever he was, it would be better to seem asleep, or unconscious. He knew this instinctively.

"Is he awake?" A voice asked.

That was—

"No," he identified Cian's voice. "I am not surprised. He's been under my personal supervision, with the help of your mage. While we can't kill him yet, his stay here doesn't need to be pleasant." Cian laughed.

Brennan was struck again at the childlike petulance of Cian's words. A grown man who couldn't seem to behave like one. Iris was right. He'd never grown up. How was that possible? Apparently, he'd learned something of intrigue and what it took to foster a rebellion.

"That is too bad," the first voice said. "I should have liked to have spoken with him."

Ailla. Ailla was here.

"Why? What could you possibly have to say to him?"

Brennan could hear the naked jealousy in Cian's question. Did the man have any pride whatsoever?

"Oh, darling," he heard her sigh, "One always enjoys a little triumph over one's opponent. Don't you agree?"

"You're not to come in here without me," Cian said.

Obviously, Cian's feelings were not soothed by Ailla's words. He was jealous and didn't manage it well. It was something to take note of. Interesting, too, as he was involved with Dhysara. Apparently, fidelity only went one way with Cian.

"What are you doing now?" Ailla asked.

Brennan could hear a note in her voice that hadn't been there previously. It didn't bode well for him.

"I'm draining him," Cian sounded gleeful. "I shall keep him alive long enough to see us succeed, but I might as well get something for my effort in not just killing him. He has magic, and I shall have it."

"You managed it!" Ailla's voice was happier than he'd ever heard it. What did she see in this small, little man? Why were they after his magic? "I was concerned that you'd kill him before you found the correct way."

"Of course I managed it. I have the old magic, and that is all one needs," Cian said. His voice held certainty.

For the first time, Brennan felt fear.

Iris

"*W*hat has she heard?" I moved closer to Jharak, wanting to make sure I didn't miss a thing.

"Do you trust her to tell you the truth?" Drake asked at the same time.

Jharak held up a hand. "A moment, if you please. I practically ran down here, and I am not as young as I used to be."

"Or thinking up a good way to tell us the bad news," Drake muttered.

"Have a seat," I stepped back, allowing Jharak to come into the study.

He chose a chair and fell into it. I sat across from

him. Drake moved behind me, and I could feel him pacing. Probably had his arms crossed too, trying to look all bad ass. I wanted to tell him that routinely didn't work with your dad, but people needed to figure those things out for themselves.

"What does Cian say? Why did he get in touch with Nerida?" I asked.

"He wants his mommy," Drake sneered.

"Well, it's reasonable. Most people are rather attached to their parents," Jharak said in a mild tone. "I rather think it's because he feels he can both hurt and scare her the most—a two for one sort of thing. If that's the case, it's working. She contacted me via the mirror, and she was crying. I haven't seen her cry since you said you wanted to stay with us," he said to Drake.

"Oh, that made her happy?" Drake wasn't giving an inch.

I'd heard about the run-in with Nerida, and the hate she'd thrown at Drake. Like he wanted to be a replacement for her asshat kid Cian? Like anyone wanted that? But she'd thrown it anyway.

"Of course it did," Jharak snapped. "We were both very happy. You'll have time to fight it out with her later. Ignore her hateful words, and see where they are coming from. Nerida has never dealt with the reality of losing Cian. Now she must, and her two younger sons are in danger. She is in a quandary. She's not behaving well; I realize that—but allow for the circumstances, if you please."

"That's asking a lot, in my opinion," I started.

"No one did," Jharak snapped.

Oooh, he had a temper. Now I could see where Brennan got his. I'd always seen Jharak as reasonable and level-headed. I stifled a laugh. These fae thought they were above all the humans in terms of...well, just about everything. But they were just as bad as we were. I decided to keep that observation to myself, however. I also overlooked Jharak's rudeness. He'd never been rude to me before. I would bet this was the stress talking.

"Cian has told her that if we agree to let him keep Brennan, and return him to his birthright as the Fae King, with us stepping down immediately, of course, he will pursue no further acts against us."

"That's it?" I asked, leaping up. "That's his offer? Did she tell him to pound sand?"

"She let him know she would relay the message to me. I am telling you so that you know where you stand when you catch up with him."

"Why does he want Brennan?"

"Nerida asked him to return Brennan, and he told her that was not open for discussion. So you must find him. There is no other way."

"Can you find him via magic? Spells he's using? Or anything like that?" I demanded.

Jharak shook his head. "No, I am sorry, Iris. You will have to find him the old-fashioned way."

"I welcome it." Drake's voice was hard behind me.

I whirled around. "I don't! How long will he keep Brennan alive? If he's even still alive?" My words fell off as the thought of him gone hit me, and I struggled not to cry.

"We will find him, and find him alive, Iris," Drake strode towards me. "I promise you. I will not let him die at the hand of that bastard."

"Tell Nerida to stall Cian," I said slowly, turning back to Jharak. "Or have her plead for Brennan's life. Tell her to cry and carry on like her life depended on it." I kept all the snarky remarks back.

"I will do so, in order to give you more time," Jharak said. "But I must tell you I don't think time is on our side. You will need to hurry."

Drake nodded as he walked towards his father. "We will. Keep him occupied. Iris," he glanced at me briefly. "Do you need anything else?"

"No. I got everything I needed before. I just have to toss it all in my bag."

"Then go and get it together. Father, let's check the horses and provisions. I'll meet you back here shortly, Iris." He walked to the door, expecting Jharak to follow.

But he didn't. Jharak looked at me and then spoke. "You do not have to do this, Iris. Drake and Taranath will not allow anything to happen to Brennan. You can stay here, and I will keep you safe."

I was shaking my head before he even finished. "There is no way in hell I am staying here. I am going to find my husband and kill the people who took him." It wasn't as hard saying it this time. Knowing that Cian would never give him back had broken something in me. It was all I could do not to drop in a heap and wail like a little kid. I could feel my heart racing and my head ringing.

With anger. I wanted to hurt Cian and Ailla so badly they never got up off the ground again.

"Where do you go first?" Jharak asked Drake.

"The Dwarf Realm, to the cottage where we found Cian with Dhysara. She lives there now, and while people know she has her husband, Kelan, as he's been known, with her at times, people near them think he is a traveling scholar, and that is why he is not at home all the time. She is a haven for him. We need to take that away."

Jharak nodded and reached out to me. I let him take my hand. He squeezed it, and then said, in a low tone, "You will get him back, Iris."

"Is that a promise?" I asked, hoping my voice didn't

waver. I didn't want my anger to be mistaken for fear or hysterics.

"No, a feeling. I will see you shortly," Jharak replied, and then he and Drake left, and I was alone in the study.

———

*H*alf an hour later, they were back. I'd finished packing everything up, including what passed for toiletries in Fae. I would need to work on this later. The ladies were missing out here.

"We're ready," Drake announced. "Give me your bags, Iris."

I stood, holding out the one sea bag I'd brought from home.

"That's it?"

"I know how to pack light."

"That will make your horse happier," Jharak smiled at me. "I will take my leave of you here. I don't want to make a big fanfare of your leaving. It will only give gossips more to spread." He came towards me and stopped when he was in front of me. Then he held out his hands towards me.

Drake took my bag and hoping I was doing the right thing; I held my hands towards Jharak. He took them, and I marveled at how soft and firm his grip felt.

"I promise you, daughter, that I shall do all I can to help return my son to you and his Realm," Jharak said formally.

Oh, shit. Was this some sort of thing? I had no idea what to do. He'd never called me daughter before, and this had the air of formality. I shot a panicked glance at Drake.

"Accept my pledge, Iris," Jharak said softly.

"I...I accept your pledge," I said. God, could I sound any dorkier?

He squeezed my hands, and he was the Jharak I knew once more. "Excellent. Know that in spite of Nerida, I will not let my son die at the hands of Cian."

I noted that he didn't call Cian his son. That was progress.

"We need to go," Drake said.

"Where's Taranath?"

"He's waiting for us in the courtyard."

I smiled at Jharak, hoping I looked reassuring. Then I followed Drake to the door.

"Bring him back," Jharak said. "We'll make everything right from there."

For whatever reason, his words, the way he said them, something—brought a lump to my throat, and I couldn't answer. I nodded, and turned, walking out the door.

If we didn't succeed...I couldn't think of that.

We'd get him back.

Or die trying.

I followed Drake down the corridor, and then the steps. We reached the courtyard without running into anyone. That was odd but a good thing. We needed to keep this low key.

Taranath stood by a group of three horses. Shit. I hadn't ridden a horse in a long time —not since we'd spent a long winter in the Bahamas. I hoped I wouldn't fall on my ass, or anything else embarrassing.

"You do know how to ride?" Drake stopped suddenly.

"Little late to ask now, don't you think?" I walked around him. "Yes, although it's been a while."

He caught up to me, pointing at the gray horse closest to us. "This one is yours. She's fast but calm. Just follow us, and she'll do well."

"What's her name?" I asked.

"Her name?" He grinned. "The name of a great Fae Queen—at least to you humans. Morgana."

I stroked her forehead and down to her muzzle. She gave me the side eye. "Look, you be easy with me, and I'll do the same," I said to her. "Deal?"

Drake snickered behind me.

"Shut it," I said. "Can I get a boost?"

Without speaking, he came closer and held his hands together with fingers laced for me to step into.

Praying I didn't look stupid, I stepped up, and he lifted, giving me the clearance I needed to swing onto Morgana's back. She shuffled her feet a little with me, and then stopped as I grabbed the reins.

One hurdle down. I wiggled in the saddle a bit. Oh boy. I was going to be sore tonight.

I was very glad at that moment that I'd changed into jeans. A dress with loose fabric would make things worse for me. I was also glad no one was offering comment on my clothes. Maybe Drake had warned everyone beforehand.

"Where's my bag?" I asked, twisting a little to see the others.

"I have it on my horse. Don't worry; I won't lose your clothes, ladyship."

"Good thing," I turned back around. "I might have to hurt you."

"You could try," Drake said.

We both laughed.

"A journey that begins with laughter is one that will be successful," Taranath said quietly.

"Well, let's hope that's right," I said.

Drake didn't say anything, just nudged his horse and headed for the front gate.

Without another word, Taranath and I followed.

4

Iris

We rode in silence for about ten minutes. I couldn't stand the silence any longer, and asked, "Why are we on horses? Why can't we just portal?" I don't know why this hadn't occurred to me before.

"Because our enemies can trace us via our use of portals," Taranath said.

"So we have to do this the non-magic way," Drake grumbled.

"My butt won't thank you for that," I said.

Silence greeted my words. Maybe that was too much? Oh, well.

"It's been a long time since I've been on a horse for any duration," Taranath finally offered.

"Well, good. I hate to be the only one suffering at the end of the day. So what—or rather, how far do you think we can get today?"

"Well, we should be on the borders of the Goblin Realm by day's end," Drake said. "Barring anything out of the ordinary."

The Goblin Realm was bigger than I thought. It seemed immense when you couldn't travel with a portal and have this over in a snap.

"We are also taking the roads less traveled," Taranath added.

I giggled. They wouldn't get it, so I tried to keep it quiet. It was hard. Things that I found funny as a human were often lost on my new fae family. I looked around. The dark of the woods all around us seemed huge, and all noise was amplified.

"I'm not even going to ask," Drake sighed. "However, if you have questions, this would be a good time to ask, Iris."

"So how does Cian keep this up? He's married to Dhysara, right?"

"Yes," Drake replied.

"Doesn't Ailla know about that? She doesn't seem the type to share. And what does Dhysara know?"

"That is an excellent question," Taranath answered

this time. "We are not sure what she knows. In my opinion, she and Cian moved to the Dwarf Realm to keep her innocent of anything else Cian planned."

"Can't romance another woman once you get married," Drake interrupted. "Kind of puts a damper on things."

That made me laugh again, and this time, I didn't hide it. "So he's a big old manipulator. We knew that, though. I wonder why Ailla puts up with it."

"What do you mean?" Taranath sounded interested.

I was glad Drake hadn't asked. "Like I said, she doesn't seem the type to share. She has no choice to share in this case. I mean, look at how she reacted to me. She has an agenda, sure, but she was pissed at me. That was just her being her."

"You can't know that," Drake said.

"Oh, women know." I knew a jealous bitch when I saw one.

"Forgive me, but I have to disagree," Drake replied.

I shrugged, even though he couldn't see me. "Okay. Maybe you're right, and I'm wrong."

He laughed. "But you don't think so?"

"Nope. Anyway, what are we expecting with Dhysara?" I didn't want to argue with him, and thinking about what lay ahead was a good distraction. Meeting her would make this all real. You'd think me bouncing along on a horse would make it real, but it didn't feel like it. Not yet. Not unless I thought about Brennan. He should be here with me.

I will not cry, I will not cry, I will not cry, I thought. I inhaled and told myself to hold it together, as Drake started to speak. I needed to pay attention.

"I don't know. She was ferocious when we attempted to catch Cian earlier. She's skilled in the magical arts, so you need to let Taranath and I take the lead. I don't want you hurt, Iris."

"But—"

"Brennan would have my head and other body parts should I allow any harm come to you. Will you please trust me on this? Please? Part of my responsibility is to keep the King and Queen safe. I will not shut you out, or keep you from anything, but I am asking if you will help me to meet my responsibilities?"

I started to speak and stopped. I could hear the sincerity in Drake's words. He might piss me off, but he didn't want me hurt, any more than he wanted Brennan hurt. To think otherwise was an insult to him, and to his honor. I knew this without being told.

"Yes, I will hang back. I have one favor to ask you all, though. Will you please work with me on a couple of spells so that I am not completely helpless against all these people who know more than I do?"

"You already know more than you think, your

Majesty," Taranath said in his mild tone. "You merely need to have more faith and pay attention."

"Well, it has been a bit of a crazy town around here," I groused, stung by the bit about not paying attention. That and I could already tell my butt was going to hurt like mad tonight.

"True, but you need to allow yourself to work with what you do know," and I heard the voice of my teacher-slash-taskmaster.

I sighed. I wasn't going to win this. "All right. Let's go over it, shall we? Since we have a long ride today." I looked up. It was going to be long. We'd left when it was still dark, and the sun was only just rising over the horizon.

A really, really long day.

———

$\mathcal{W}$ hen we stopped for lunch, I was ready to never look at a horse again. Morgana was a great horse, and very easy, but as suspected, my backside was suffering.

"Oh, wow, I needed to get off and stretch," I said, rubbing my lower back.

Drake gave me a contemptuous look. "Such a softie."

"Shut it, sword boy," I shot back. He had been on

me the entire morning, teasing and taunting to the point that Taranath told him to zip it. That had been worth the harassment.

"Shall we eat?" Taranath asked.

I was so glad he was with us. Not only because he was superb at what he did, but he kept Drake and me from killing one another.

I didn't want to admit it, but Drake and I were a lot alike. I could see why Brennan had chosen me, given that this was the person that he spent most of his time with. Drake and I were two sides of the same coin. It made me like him better, although it didn't stop me from wanting to brain him.

We ate from a bag of provisions in silence. The bread, which I knew came freshly baked from the kitchens that morning, was delicious. So was the cheese.

"Do we make the cheese in the castle?" I asked. Maybe I could make some requests...

"We grow or make all our own food," Drake said proudly.

The way he said it made me think that wasn't the case everywhere. So I asked.

"No," he said. "Not all Realms can support what is needed to grow their food. There are complex trading arrangements, and sometimes, those skilled in the production of food, and some of the mages will visit other realms and help them make their Realm more productive. That's due to Brennan," he said, and I heard the pride again.

"What do you mean?"

"When he became King, if you couldn't produce your food, you just traded for it. There were no plan or efforts into changing that. He and I traveled through all the Realms right before he was crowned, and I mentioned that in the Human Realm, people worked to make the land work for them, rather than merely accepting it. That it might be possible to improve the lives of those in all the Realms. That is one reason they are all very loyal to him," he added. "All the kings who were in place when Brennan became the Goblin King remember how he shared information, and gave to them freely, with no expectation of payment or anything in return. Fae have long memories," he said, and a shadow passed his face.

I wondered at that but thought prying might not be welcomed. Drake had been honest with me. I didn't want to mess up what felt like a nice start to a new chapter in our relationship. Because we had to have one. Or we'd be fighting over Brennan. I could see that clear as day.

"Then why don't we just tell them that Cian is back, no he didn't die, and we need your help to kick Cian's ass?" I asked. I was missing something here.

"As grateful as they are, there is an element of opportunistic enthusiasm that can't be denied," Taranath said. "We have to make sure that Brennan doesn't appear weak. If he does, other Realms will feel justified in taking over the Goblin Realm."

"But they can't manage it!" I exclaimed, thinking on what Brennan had told me about the magic of all the Realms. "It'll all go downhill fast!"

Taranath nodded. "Correct. I'm glad to see the King has brought you into his confidence. They cannot hold the Goblin Throne, although none realize it."

"Oh, jeez, the place would fall apart." The various scenarios were horrifying.

"Yes, which is why we're sneaking around. We need to get him back, and put Father back in the Fae Court, and put the threat of Cian away once and for all."

I could hear the steel in Drake's voice.

A thought occurred to me, and I got up and went to my bag. I hadn't been carrying the mirror Brennan gave me on my person, but it was with me at all times.

"What are you doing, Iris?" Drake came up behind me.

"Do you think they took his mirror?"

"They would be foolish not to."

"Would they even know to look for it?" I asked.

Drake shared a look with Taranath and then came back to me. "I don't know."

I couldn't tell what was going on in his head. "What do you mean? What aren't you telling me?"

"I'm honest, Iris. I don't know. I'm not sure if Cian would know that Brennan carried one—do you know if he had his on him at the moment he was taken?"

I felt the heat rise in my cheeks, and my heart began to pound when I thought about what had been going on when the asshole burst in. We were in bed together. Nowhere to hide a mirror.

"Well, we'd only just woken. If he had time to grab it—I don't know. Someone grabbed me and knocked me out. Not with a punch, or anything!" I saw them both come towards me with expressions of worry. "But everything went black until I woke and saw that Brennan was gone. You know," I added, "I am getting pretty sick of being knocked out with the magic punch when it's convenient for everyone else."

Drake and Taranath both smiled.

"Then that is where our next lesson shall be," Taranath said. "We will make sure that no one can do this to you again."

"But he might have the mirror?"

I hated to dash the hope that I could hear in Drake's question. "It's possible. I don't know. I don't know anything." I held the mirror in my hand, afraid to speak to it, afraid to put it away without even trying.

"Give it to me. Better that anyone else who

might see this see me rather than you. We don't want to advertise that you are no longer in the Castle," Drake said, reaching over me to get the mirror.

I reluctantly let him take it. I didn't like to let it go to anyone else, even though I could see sense in what he said.

"Bren?" He asked quietly.

Nothing.

"Brennan?" A little louder.

Still...nothing. I could tell all three of us held our breaths, and everyone moved closer to Drake and the mirror in his hand.

"Brennan?" Drake's voice was firm. No more hiding then.

He hissed.

"What? What is it?" I wanted to grab the mirror.

"There's something moving in the mirror, even though it's dark. Like it's bouncing around."

I stared at the mirror, frustrated. Something nagged at the back of my head...what was it?

"Will you let me see it for a moment?" I asked Drake, trying to keep myself calm.

He handed it over slowly.

"Brennan, is this your 'stuck on the boat moment?'" I asked.

I could see the darkness wiggle. As though it was in

a pocket, and he couldn't get to it. Just like me, when I'd been on the boat.

"We're coming," I whispered. "I love you."

Drake snatched it as the mirror went slack in my hands.

"Be strong, brother. We're coming." He put the mirror into his pocket.

"Hey! That's mine!" Although I was glad he'd saved it from being dropped.

He took it from his pocket immediately and held it out. "I wanted to end the connection. He's not able to get to it, but he heard it. Is that what you think?"

I shook my head a little, trying to clear it. Everything happened so quickly, and then here Drake was, asking my opinion.

"When I was out with my parents and Mara and Heath, Brennan called me. I couldn't answer at the moment, so I tapped on the mirror to let him know I had heard him. We had a big fight about it," I could feel the tears in my eyes, and my throat hurt, trying to keep myself from fighting.

"Well done, your Majesty. We know that he's alive," Taranath came closer and patted me on the shoulder. "That is a step in the right direction."

"Do we even know it's him?" I asked, my voice breaking.

Drake smiled, and I could see the animal side of

him. "It doesn't matter, does it? If it's in the hands of someone else, I would think they would have responded in some manner. Even if they had the sense not to, we know he's there. With the mirror. No one else could have taken it from his chamber. So we are aware that we're in the right direction."

"Yeah, but where is the right direction?" I shouted, not caring that we were supposed to be discreet.

"First, the Dwarf Realm to see what Dhysara knows, and then we make our decision from there."

The look on Drake's face didn't bode well for Dhysara. I knew I ought to be more bothered, but I wasn't. Her man had taken mine and planned to kill him. I had to save my sympathy for those not trying to kill me or those I loved.

"Let's go," Drake said.

I tucked the mirror into my back pocket, not wanting to put it back in the bag and lose my connection with Brennan.

The three of us cleaned up the meal quickly and in silence. Then after a boost for me, we rode back onto the road.

Brennan was alive! Please, please, please, let him still be alive!

Brennan

*H*e felt the mirror vibrate and did his best to tap the mirror discreetly. He heard...it was Drake! Drake had gotten the mirror from Iris! He rubbed his finger across where the mirror lay in his pocket, watching as much as he could at Cian across the room.

He couldn't see what the bastard was doing, but it wasn't good. It would probably hurt. But he felt hope as he'd not felt in days. Drake had located him. Knew he was alive. Which meant that Drake would not stop until he'd found Brennan and killed Cian.

The thought made him smile through cracked lips. He was thirsty, and he'd learned that water would not be given to him regularly. Not here.

"Brennan, is this your 'stuck on the boat moment?'" Her voice whispered across him like the sweetest wind. Iris! He almost smiled at the memory of the time when she'd been out on her parents' boat. She'd been unable to talk when he called her. It was clever, her asking in that manner.

She was alive, and well. He tapped at the mirror again, shuffling his feet as he did so to keep Cian hearing the voices in his pocket. It wouldn't do to lose the mirror now.

"We're coming. I love you," Iris said.

Then Drake spoke. "Be strong, brother. We're coming."

Hope and panic flared through him sharper than any of the pain that Cian had inflicted so far. They couldn't come! The thought of rescue was intoxicating, but if Iris came here, Cian would hurt her, kill her, and his life would be over.

Even these thoughts didn't dampen the hope that hearing the voices of the two people he loved most.

He must have smiled once more. He didn't realize it and cursed himself when Cian approached him, an evil grin in place.

"What is so amusing, brother? Is this too gentle? Well, we shall have to address that, won't we?"

With a laugh, Cian moved out of Brennan's eyesight, and Brennan closed his eyes.

5

Iris

*O*nce we were going again, I didn't try and stop the tears. He was alive. It could be someone else, but I knew, with everything I had, that he was alive. And he'd heard me. I hoped it would give him strength—for whatever he was going through. The thought of Cian hurting him made me cry harder and want to kill the guy all at once.

Taranath rode up beside me. "Please, your Majesty, take this." He held out a small square of cloth.

I took it and mopped at my face. I wanted to blow my nose, but that would ruin the thing forever.

Taranath always had something like mind-reading going on. "It's yours to keep. It washes easily, and we'll be able to do that tonight if needed." He smiled at me and rode ahead to the space next to Drake.

I blew my nose. No sense in being snotty while ugly crying. I had a sneaking suspicion that it wouldn't be the last time I cried. It would, however, be the last time I cried in front of anyone else. I didn't know what the protocol was but having met Nerida, and Ailla—these royal families didn't cry in front of other people. What was it Brennan had told me? That fae rarely cried at all. So I needed to confine my tears.

That might be hard. Practicing keeping it together around a friendly audience would be best. I inhaled deeply and pulled my shoulders back. Well, as best I could while riding a horse.

And a horse! What the hell? I hadn't expected this when I thought about traveling. I wished we could portal, but I trusted that Drake and Taranath were making the best choice to allow us to sneak around.

We rode in silence, all lost in our thoughts. I wondered what we were in for when we found Dhysara. Brennan told me that she seemed very protective of Cian and that he'd behaved in a way that said he cared for her—so what was he doing with Ailla the psycho?

Well, he was a psycho as well, so there was that. I felt the brief swelling of sympathy for her,

remembering Drake's expression when talking
about her.

The silence was broken by Taranath. "Your Majesty,
would you like to go over some of the spells we've been
practicing?"

"Can I practice on Drake?"

I saw the twitch of the shoulders in front of me and
smiled.

Taranath smiled a little. "Well, he's probably not
the best target, your Majesty. We might have need of
him later."

Even I didn't miss the snort from Drake. I'd been
worried that this would be uncomfortable, and in spite
of my backside concerns, it was nice to discover that
traveling with these two wasn't horrible.

If one could forget why we had to go in the first
place. Which I couldn't. It lurked there, in the back of
my mind.

Thoughts of how this would help Brennan in the
end, no matter how tedious Taranath could be on
doing things right, kept me focused as he and I walked
through what I'd learned so far.

That night, we stopped and made a little camp off
the road we'd been on all day. I fell asleep instantly,
Brennan's face in my mind.

Please be all right, I thought. To whom, I didn't
know. I could almost feel him next to me, his presence,

his smell. I missed him so badly at that moment; I nearly cried out. Where are you? I thought. Please be all right.

I could hear the breathing of the others slow and deepen. I lay on the hard ground, missing my husband. The ground didn't bother me—I'd slept outside plenty of times when we traveled. The deck of the boat was just as unforgiving as the ground. That wasn't what kept me awake.

It was worry, and how wrong this felt to be here, without Brennan. Not that I didn't care for both Drake and Taranath. There was no one else I'd rather have with me to go and find Brennan. It was that I wasn't with him, and it made me feel off-kilter.

I'd felt this way all day, but between worry and my aching backside, I didn't have the time or the luxury to mull it over.

The night sounded different here, too. There was no water, and in spite of being on land while Mom was undergoing treatment, I was used to going to sleep with the sound of water in the background. It hadn't been as noticeable or as bad when I was Brennan. His presence brought me a comfort, a sense of security that it was okay that I didn't have all the things I was used to.

But now, with him missing, and me being unsure when we'd get him back, or what shape he'd be in—I couldn't contemplate any other outcome—all the things that were so different from what I was used to looming large.

I rolled away from the small fire, pulling my blanket up and trying to muffle my tears. I had to be strong.

Tomorrow, I would be. Now, I let the tears fall and missed my husband.

I must have fallen asleep. When I woke, I wasn't lying on the ground, nor was I huddled near a fire. I was...I was back in my—our—room in the Goblin Castle.

"Brennan?" I called.

He came from the darkness, a smile on his face that made my toes tingle. "I am here, my love." He slid onto the bed. The moon shone through the window opposite our bed, a pathway for him to move up towards me.

I opened my arms, welcoming him.

"I missed you, wife," he said.

His arms went around me, bands of steel that both excited me, and made me melt with desire. They traveled up to my shoulders, gently tugging on the scalloped edge of my nightgown.

"You are wearing far too much," his voice breathed into my ear.

"Then please help me fix that," I whispered back.

He drew the nightgown over my head, letting it fall off to the side. My arms were raised, and he ran his hands down the underside of my arms. I could feel all my skin rippled with goosebumps at his touch.

"You are so lovely. I cannot believe that you are mine," Brennan met my eyes.

I fell into them. How could I resist? Blazing pools of blue, and bright in the moonlight. Could he get any better?

"I feel the same way. Would you please carry on?" I asked, wanting-not-wanting to laugh.

He chuckled, and bent his head to my neck, kissing me precisely with agonizing slowness. When he reached my collarbone, he nipped at it.

I felt my body arch towards him. Who knew the collarbone would make me want to claw my way inside of him? I felt the dampness between my legs increase. It was obvious that he planned to toy with me, make me beg.

I couldn't wait.

Without warning, the room went dark, and it felt as though a bag had been shoved over my head, and I felt Brennan—his arms, his hands, his mouth, all of him—ripped from me.

"Brennan!" I screamed.

I sat up and saw that Drake had jumped out of his bedding to hurry towards me.

"What is it?" he asked.

I couldn't help it, in spite of my earlier vow. I started to cry, the tears interfering with speaking. "I...I had a dream. We were back in the Castle, and none of this..." I stopped as the tears overtook me.

Drake patted me awkwardly on the shoulder. "I'm sorry, Iris. We're going to find him. Try to get some sleep. We have a few more hours still."

He and Taranath, who had also woken up, but left matters to Drake, crawled back into their bedding. I lay down once more, the tears leaking into my blankets.

How was I supposed to sleep after that?

Brennan

He woke, his body arched in a spasm that was painful. The room was dark and other than his gasping; there were no other sounds. He could hear the beating of his heart, a strong thump that rang in his ears.

He'd been dreaming. But of what?

Iris.

The one word made his entire body burst into flames. He'd been touching her, pulling her nightdress from her.

Then...nothing.

He sighed. There was no way he'd be able to go back to sleep now. But he needed to try. Each day brought a test of endurance. Sleep was one of the few things keeping him going.

He closed his eyes, but all he could see was Iris. When would he see her again?

6

Iris

When I woke, I could feel that my body wasn't happy at this sleeping on the ground thing. I sat up and stretched. My butt hurt, as expected. My eyes felt dry and scratchy. I'd cried for a long time after I woke from my dream. Be strong, I told myself. Brennan needs you to be strong. You have to be as strong as Taranath and Drake. You can do this.

"Taranath?" I asked.

"Yes?" He was behind me, somewhere.

"You got anything for aches?" I hoped that my eyes and heart fell into the aches category.

He laughed. "I can help, I think."

"Thank God," I breathed. Why hadn't I thought of

this yesterday? For all his talk of being serious when using magic, if it helped my aching backside as well as my other hurts I would take the heat for breaking the rules. Which brought another thought to mind.

"Taranath?" I asked again.

"Are you in need of assistance at this moment?"

"Yeah, whenever, but no, I had another question." I tried smiling and hoped he didn't notice my face. I needed to think about something else other than the Brennan of my dream I saw every time I closed my eyes.

"Yes?"

I saw that Drake was busy over a small fire, cooking something that smelled good. This was like camping. So much for the advanced ways of the fae, I thought to myself with a snicker. We lived easier on the boat.

"We were talking about the cost of magic yesterday, and I was wondering how Cian, and Ailla, and her dad, and whoever else, was managing with this *there's a cost for everything* idea," I sat down near Drake. He was also making tea, which was the preferred hot beverage here. I'd take it.

As if reading my mind, which he probably was in a sorta-kinda way, Drake handed me a cup. I wrapped my hands around it carefully.

Taranath finally spoke. "I don't know. There is a cost to all that we do, as there are consequences for everything. Perhaps that is why Cian still carries his physical scars. He is not a good person and hurts others. He could heal via magic, most fae do. But he hasn't. I honestly do not know. As I have told Drake, and the Fae King, there is much here that is being used that is old, and not well known."

"The dragon magic?" I asked.

"Perhaps. Dragons were the most dangerous with or without their magic. However, there are many forms of magic which have been lost or are not in everyday use. Most fae use magic to make daily life easier, and that's about it. While we're all concerned with it, it's not something the majority of those in the Realms worry over."

"Wouldn't that be nice?" I sighed. The thought of all I—we—didn't know gave me lots of worries.

Another thought struck. "What do you think will happen if Dhysara is there?" I asked.

This time, Drake answered. "I don't have the impression that she is like Ailla, going by the reports I've heard. She was very fierce in her defense of Cian when Brennan and I tried to apprehend him but—"

"Even though he's nutters I can understand being fierce in defense of those you care for," I interjected.

Drake nodded. "That's my thought as well. If he's not there, and I don't think he would be, since my intelligence suggests that Dhysara is not aware of how close Ailla and Cian are, she may be reasonable. I suspect, although I could be wrong, that she may not even know that he's taken Brennan."

"I hope not." I was feeling bad for my lack of charity the night before towards her. "But if we're wrong—"

"Then she shares the fate of all who are allied with Cian," Drake said in a hard voice.

There was no arguing with that. We ate in silence, and when the little camp had been packed, we mounted up—after a little healing spell shot towards me, thank God—and rode away.

I tried to calm the butterflies in my stomach. We'd reach the cottage in the Dwarf Realm today. I hoped it wouldn't be a repeat of the last time. From what Brennan had told me, it had been a near thing, and Cian had hurt him. I hoped Cian wouldn't be there.

Brennan

*T*he dark brought comfort. For the moment, it meant that no one was trying to hurt him. When he'd been younger, some of his training had concerned times like this—how to withstand pain and make it to the other side. But that was long ago, and he felt the strain of protecting himself from Cian. Of protecting Iris, and all he loved, from Cian.

It took him several days—what he thought was several days—to decipher what Cian planned. He wanted Brennan's magic.

Without warning, a memory from the time before swept him up. A time when they were still children. Before Cian had been hurt, but after everything changed.

"You're not special. You're nothing at all," Cian's voice hissed.

Brennan lay in the dark, hands behind his head. He'd been going over the lessons of the day, and where he'd made so many mistakes.

He and Cian no longer shared rooms. What was Cian doing here in his rooms? How had he gotten in without making any noise?

"I'm tired, Cian. Leave me alone." He didn't want to argue.

"I saw you today, parading around with all your new teachers," Cian continued as though he hadn't spoken. "Talking like you were one of them. You're not. You're nothing. You'll never be anything other than the Goblin King!"

"That's why I have lessons. Being the Goblin King has different responsibilities than those of the Fae King."

"Of course it does," Cian sneered, a snicker breaking out in his voice. "Because you're going to have to deal with nasty goblins and probably a nasty goblin wife. I'd need magic lessons too!" His voice changed, and Brennan felt fear. "Don't ever think you'll be more than me. I will be King of all the Realms! You'll die in that nasty goblin-infested pest hole! And so you don't forget," A light flared, and Brennan felt a sting on his face, "This is just a taste of what will happen if you do."

He rubbed his face and his eyes, trying not to cry out. Not only from the obvious pain but how hard had Cian's words hit him. What had happened to his brother? They'd always been the best of friends. But Cian treated him as an enemy now.

Once the pain began to subside, he listened. He was alone again. He waited a few moments more, to be sure.

Only then did he let tears come. When would this end?

It had never ended, Brennan realized as the memory faded. All those years, he'd thought Cian dead, and himself at some resolution with the matter. No peace, but a resolution that he couldn't change his past. It's why he'd tried hard to make his Realm better, make relations with the surrounding Realms better. To keep women from getting too close, because he never wanted to hurt another ever again. All his life he'd tried to be better than that time from his childhood.

When in reality, he'd never been as bad as he thought, and Cian had always been there. Still angry, still plotting, and still a spoiled, bratty, over-indulged mean child.

Cian now was no different than the Cian he'd known over six hundred years ago. It was tragic that Cian hadn't chosen to change himself, and enjoy being alive, and apparently loved by two women, both of whom were strong, impressive women. Ailla was horrid, but she was not weak. Dhysara loved him in a way that Brennan would have envied before he'd found Iris.

And yet all the man wanted to do was exact revenge for old hurts that were not even real. Cian didn't seem to care that he'd toss all the Realms into complete upheaval. Brennan knew, even if Cian couldn't see it, and he doubted that his brother could, due to the madness upon him, that the Realms would not survive what Cian had planned.

They would revolt, and their entire world would fall into the chaos of war and killing. A man would understand it. Cian was not a man. A madman, perhaps, but a man like himself, or Drake? No.

That meant that the reason and method of dealing with another man would not work. He would need to remember that in all dealings that would come. He must be the parent, the adult, and treat Cian as a child.

Because that was what he was. An angry, petulant child who cared nothing for others as long as he got what he wanted. It would do no good to warn of what would come of Cian's plans. Another adult—he might have a chance of showing the consequences. But Cian didn't care.

He had to live. He had to survive this. Not only for Iris, and the life they planned but for Drake. His Realm. All the other Realms that had no part in the tragedy of his family. For his parents, even his mother.

In spite of the physical hurts, in spite of how very tired he felt, a burden had fallen from him. He was not responsible for Cian's death. Although if he had anything to do with it when it occurred now, he would be in the end. But what had gone on all those years ago, that was not his fault. His brother had not died. His parents had made a decision that was in poor judgment, but that was not his fault either. They should have told him the truth, corrected what he thought he knew about Cian. They did not.

He had done all that he could for his entire life to make amends for his actions, and in doing so, had become a good ruler, and a good man. He no longer needed to carry the sins of the past with him as part of his armor.

Why had it taken all this time to get to this understanding? Even with his parents' deception, he could have let this go long ago.

A sliver of light from the side of the room reflected on the ceiling. Then the light disappeared. He felt the presence of someone in the chamber, but there was no noise.

"May as well show yourself," he said, letting his voice sound unconcerned.

"Shhh," a voice—a woman?—responded. "I can help you, but I don't have much time."

"How?" He whispered.

"Be quiet," the woman said, and she sounded irritated. "Don't look askew at good fortune."

"Be assured, madam, I do not." Unspoken was the question as to whether this was, in fact, good fortune. He hoped so. But beggars could not be choosy, and if she were here to help him, he'd ask no questions. Couldn't be much worse than what Cian was doing to him daily. He was weakening. He could feel it.

A greenish glow came close to him, and he could see, by turning his head, a small, dark woman's face. Well, her hair and clothes looked dark in the light of whatever spell she was casting.

"May I ask—?"

"No." Her answer was swift.

The glow spread from her hands and moved to his

middle. The pool of glowing green light grew as it moved through his core, and he felt as though someone had injected sunlight through him.

"Good, let it all heal you. I can try and come to you as long as you are here if you can keep your mouth shut," she said, still sounding irritated.

Was it that hard to be decent? He wondered. This was probably not the time to be particular.

When it felt that he could break free of his restraints and fly with the birds, the light faded from his middle, and from her hands. She blew a breath onto her hands, and a small red flame sprung to life in her hand.

"You'll do," she said, peering closely at him.

He was surprised to see how young she looked. She was fae and...something else. Her features were fairer than he'd originally thought. He couldn't tell what it was, but she was not entirely fae. But her youth was in slight discordance with the weight of something that showed in her face, young as she was. If she had even reached one hundred, he'd be surprised.

"Who's Iris?" She asked abruptly.

"My wife," he said without thinking. Where had she heard Iris' name? The thought of Iris as his wife thrilled him, even as he cursed himself for answering without restraint. Had he spoken it when he dreamed of her last?

"You need to stop thinking about her," she said. "He'll see it. He's as dumb as a horse's hind end, but he is cunning. Block her from your thoughts."

The red flame winked out, and a moment later, he saw the door crack open, closing quickly.

What had that been about? Who was she? Could he trust her? The woman had healed him. Why had she warned him about thinking of Iris? He never spoke of her, rarely talked about anything when Cian was present. He found that his silence angered his brother as much as words.

It usually meant that he endured more pain than he might have if he'd given the madman something to taunt him with. Given how Cian behaved, Brennan felt keeping Iris--and all of his life--hidden was more important.

He also thanked whatever had pushed him to wed quietly. Had it been broadcast as Jharak wanted, Iris would be in further danger. They'd had a party, but it hadn't been anything near what Jharak wanted.

Although he feared she was in more danger than he'd like when he thought of her telling him they were coming. Who were they? And why in the name of all the gods had they let Iris come?

He stopped his thoughts. There was nothing he could do from where he was. He needed to take the mystery woman's words to heart, and wall his thoughts of Iris off into a place where Cian could not find them. If this mystery woman knew, who knew what Cian had discovered?

He closed his eyes. Better to get sleep while he could.

7

Iris

*D*rake reined his horse and held up a hand.

"What?" I asked.

"We are close to the cottage. Iris, please stay here. Taranath, would you see what wards are in place? I would imagine there are at least a few of them."

Taranath edged around me, looking calm as he always did. I envied that. I could feel the butterflies turn mean and swirl in my gut with all sorts of crazy intent. Intent to make me puke, maybe. Please, no. Last thing I needed.

Taranath disappeared beyond the line of trees.

"How can you tell there are wards?" I whispered, nudging Morgana closer to Drake and his horse.

He shrugged. "I can't, without looking for them specifically. But Taranath can, and it's what I would do if I were the hidden son of the Fae King." He turned to look at me and smiled, and I could see why he was considered so fierce at that moment. He almost scared me. It was a smile that was excited about the battle.

We sat still, or I tried to. I wanted to fidget. Everything on me itched, and I felt ready to jump out of my skin. Which I nearly did when Taranath appeared out of the trees.

"There were wards, but I have disabled them."

Drake peered around behind Taranath. "Will those within be aware?"

"I do not know. So I'd suggest that you take whatever action you plan to take," Taranath said, smiling at me.

How in the hell did he stay so calm? Drake moved around the two of us. "Stay behind me," he ordered. "If you could both please arm yourselves with spells to protect us that will help. I'll lead, and you follow," and without waiting for a response, he pushed through the trees.

"We can do this, your Majesty," Taranath said softly. "You've already done magic far more challenging."

"Yeah but not on purpose," I said. Still, his confidence made me feel better.

"See the spell in your mind," he turned his horse around, and we followed Drake. "Have it in front of you, and be ready to speak it."

It had taken some time for me to learn things because everything that Taranath taught me was in the fae language. But I did as he instructed, and I could see the spell words in my head that I needed for protection. I focused on protecting all of us, rather than just myself. I wanted to close my eyes to focus better, but that wouldn't work here.

Drake rode forward, his horse turning a little.

"Hello, the cottage!" He yelled. "Come out, if you please! We wish to speak with you."

No answer. It felt as the air itself waited for some response. I could feel myself holding my breath.

Then the door opened, only a sliver.

"Who are you? What do you want?"

It was a woman.

"We are in search of the man called Kelan. Is he here?" Drake sounded confident, but not overly threatening.

"What do you want with him? He's done nothing to anyone!"

Kind of defensive, wasn't she?

Drake nudged his horse, and it took a few steps closer to the cottage. A hand came through the door.

"Stop! I will not allow you to come closer. Be warned; I will protect myself and my home."

I focused on making sure that Drake stayed under my protection spell. I didn't know if it would stand up against someone more skilled, but I had to try.

As Dhysara spoke, Taranath broke away from me and rode up next to Drake. "I fear, madam, that your protection is not what you believe it to be. I have removed your wards."

The hand fell a little, then rose. "And? I do not need the wards to send you on your way."

In spite of the fact that she loved a psycho, I felt a measure of respect for her. I remembered Brennan told me that her father had been the Goblin King before he was. That must be where her strength came from. I'd be scared to death facing these two.

"I am sure you do not, but it would be better if you answered our question, madam."

The hand fell again and then withdrew inside the door. The door itself opened more, and a woman stepped out.

She had dark hair that hung loosely around her face. Not like Nerida's precisely done hair, as she was the only fae woman I had to compare her to. Well, and Ailla. Another perfectly done fae woman.

"Are you Dhysara?"

The woman stood up straight, her chin lifted and her shoulders back. "I am. Who asks?"

"I am Drake, in the service of the Goblin King. I seek Kelan, on business from my king."

A corner of her lip curled, and I could see the other two haughty fae women I'd met in her expression. "You mean the usurper? What does he have to do with me? Hasn't he done enough already? Taken my inheritance? My throne? Bespelled my father to abandon his family?"

"There is no way you could have held the Goblin Realm, Lady Dhysara," Taranath stepped in front of Drake.

"Are you his creature as well? As if you'd say anything different," she dismissed him.

I'd thought she was simple in that she didn't have all the airs and snotty attitudes of Nerida and Ailla, but clearly, I was wrong. She wore a plain dark tunic that showed her to be a soft-looking curvy woman, in spite of her height and her presence. But she held herself like a queen.

For a moment, I felt small but remembered. I am the Goblin Queen, no matter what this woman thinks of herself, or me. I am the Queen, legally married to the King. I straightened in the saddle. If I felt less than by comparison, it was all on me, and I wasn't going to let her do that to me. I also focused on the spell, making sure neither of those with me would be hurt by her.

Her eye fell on me. "What are you doing as part of this envoy, lady? You are not..." she squinted at me. "You are not full fae, although you are in part fae. What are you? Oh..." she crossed her arms. "A human? What is a human doing here?"

That was it. "I am—"

"A representative of the Goblin King," Drake interjected. "He felt that you would feel less threatened if we had a woman with us. And this woman, the Lady Iris, is a valued member of his court. It would behoove you, Lady Dhysara, to return the courtesy that is being visited upon you."

I had to force myself not to turn and gape at Drake. This tall tale that he and Taranath were spinning had no real basis in what we'd talked about, but they were doing well at making this shit up on the fly.

She looked at me, eyebrows raised. "Is that so? What does a human have to offer the usurper?"

"He is the rightful Goblin King, whatever your disagreement with him may be," I said, surprising myself with how formal I sounded. "We are here to request your help in locating Kelan."

"You were here before," her voice accused Drake. "You tried to harm him!" She backed towards the door, and the tunic she wore stretched tight across her front. My eye caught on her middle as she moved.

Drake made a movement, but I held up a hand and moved my horse in closer. I could feel my spell falter, and then the spell of another wrapped around me. Thank God. Taranath had noticed and taken up my slack. That made me feel okay about turning my attention to Dhysara. I didn't know why, but I knew this was the way to work with her. "He believed that Kelan was a threat. Now we--the King-- are unsure and need to speak with him. A simple conversation can easily clear things up," I smiled. I had a sneaking suspicion why she was worried. I watched her carefully, waiting to see if I was right.

She shifted in the door, turning so that I saw her profile. Yep, I was right. Not that I had much experience, but she had a look about her.

I slid off the horse, hoping like hell that I wouldn't fall flat on my face. My lower half still wasn't used to being on a horse for hours. "Listen, Dhysara, right? I'm Iris. We're not here to harm you. We do, however, need to find Kelan. I'm sure," I took a few steps, ignoring Drake's hiss of indrawn breath, "You would like to have him closer as well." I smiled and hoped I didn't look threatening. I also wondered why Drake couldn't tell that Taranath was all over this regarding a protection spell.

She eyed me with great suspicion, and her arms crept to her midsection, almost cradling it. I was right. How to approach this, then? I glanced quickly at Drake and Taranath; Drake hadn't noticed, but I could see Taranath studying her. He didn't miss much.

"He has felt he could not stay, couldn't put me in danger," she said slowly, reluctantly.

Her desire to know something about him warred with her need to keep his whereabouts a secret. She wasn't showing much, but the knowledge alone must have been eating at her. He wasn't here.

What had Brennan told me? Fae didn't have a lot of kids. More often than not, couples would go years without having children; so this was a big deal. I wondered if Cian knew, and thought that whatever was up with Dhysara, I couldn't help but feel sorry for her.

"Why would he feel you are in danger?" Drake asked.

His presence felt big, and I could tell that Dhysara felt it also. She shrank into the door frame a little. Not a lot, because she had a ton of pride, and that kept her back straight and her chin up, but he was intimidating.

I held my hand toward him, keeping it level. I hoped he'd get the hint and shut the hell up and ease his intimidation. Just a little.

Not waiting to see if he caught it, I took a couple of

steps closer to her, holding my hands out wide to show her that I had nothing on me and nothing to hide.

"We need to find him, Dhysara. He has been implicated in acts against the Goblin King, and he needs to answer for this. If he's not involved, no big deal, and we're all done. But we have to find him first." Please don't let her ask why Brennan is not here.

"Why has the Goblin King," she sneered, "Not come himself? He had no problem doing so once before."

"Because that didn't work out so well, did it?" I shot back. "He is willing to try a different approach. The Goblin King doesn't wish for dissent in his kingdom." I wasn't sure where I was pulling all this formality from, but it seemed appropriate. I also knew I couldn't tell her that Brennan and I were married. I had no reason as to why I felt this way, but I just knew.

She narrowed her eyes at me. "Why does he send a mage, a warrior, and a human?"

I shrugged. Interesting that she didn't mention me being part fae again. Did being part human negate that for some fae? I'd have to deal with that later, if so. "Because we volunteered, and he trusts us." Thank god that Drake and Taranath were letting me handle this. "If you can tell us where he might be, we can solve this quickly. I don't mean you any harm, particularly not now," I smiled and glanced at her belly.

She looked afraid. Then the fear slid right into anger. "Are you threatening me?"

"Not at all. I just imagine that you want him close right now, and the sooner this is handled, the better."

"You are in the service of the usurper. How can I trust you?"

"You can't," I said, feeling Taranath shifting behind me. I could feel the spell shifting. He'd need to teach me that. "But look at me—I'm here, defenseless, in front of you, and I understand you are skilled with magic, and I am only talking. That's all I want to do. Just talk, and then once that is done, we will leave."

She looked at me, then Taranath, then Drake. She didn't want to fight. "I do not know exactly where he is, but he is very close to the Dragon King. There are some who do not forget loyalty and what is right." She glared at Drake. "The king and Lady Ailla are most kind to us both."

I watched her face when she said the crazy bitch's name. She didn't know.

"Were you aware—" Drake began.

"Of any other place he might go if he felt threatened?" I interjected, turning briefly to glare at Drake. "Shut up," I hissed.

Dhysara hadn't missed that, and I saw a smirk on her face. "You take orders from the human? What have you done to be so highly regarded?" she asked me.

"She saved the king," Drake said. "Her counsel is valued."

"Oh, so the great Goblin King is poorly thought of by others? Such a surprise."

I shrugged again, determined not to let her get under my skin. In some ways, she was obviously a good match for Cian the psycho. I was beginning to question my ability to get accurate first impressions from people. "I want to make sure he is safe from harm. He has been of great help to me as well."

Dhysara laughed. "He must be if you are not dead yet."

Okay, living in the middle of nowhere had obviously let her manners fall straight into the gutter. I mean, I know that humans have a high mortality rate here. But was it totally okay to mention it like she was doing? No one else, not even Nerida, had behaved like this.

"You should return to the Human Realm and leave the affairs of the Fae Realm to your betters," she said, with no snark or anything else in her voice.

Wow. What a snotty bitch. My ability to feel sorry for her was not going to last long if she kept this up.

Calm, a voice said in my head. It sounded like Taranath. *This is merely a test. Do not let her push you.*

Definitely Taranath. I was going to have to get him to teach me this, too. Great. Like my to-do magic list wasn't long enough. But this talking in the head thing was better than the mirror. 'Extremely handy' didn't even begin to describe it.

"My betters, as you term them, are delighted to have my assistance. Do you have any reason to believe Kelan would go anywhere other than the Dragon Realm?"

She smirked for a moment, then answered. "No. I know all about him, and there is nowhere else he would go."

Yeah, she knew all about him. I took some petty satisfaction that no, she did not know all about him.

"Why do you tell us this, Mistress?" Taranath spoke for the first time. "You are no friend to my King."

She glared, and then I saw her shoulders sag a little. "Because I am tired of worrying over the usurper, and wondering when he will harm me merely because I am my father's daughter."

"He has not bothered you for more than six hundred years," Drake said, a dry tone to his words.

"Because I do not allow myself to be within his notice!" she spat. "Ever since my father was murdered, my mother and I knew we needed to protect ourselves. There was nowhere beyond the reach of the Fae King and his spawn. Nowhere. Thankfully, Eilor was kind and gave us shelter. Then he allowed Kelan and me to marry and arranged for us to live here, quietly. I will never forgive your king, but I wish to move into another part of my life and want nothing to do with him. I desire to live in peace. You may tell him that. I will not forget what he's done, but I no longer wish to be at war."

They'd never been at war. With her words, I saw what kind of life she'd had. She went to the worst place possible to have a peaceful life. Eilor and Ailla had fed the fear, and made her a little crazy. Then they got her married to Cian, the psycho, and the crazy paranoia continued. She might be a hell of a liar, but I believed her. I wished I could tell her that it was pretty likely that everyone she trusted was a big, fat lying jerk. It probably wouldn't help our situation, but I swung right back towards pity for her.

"Would you be willing to call on him, see where he is? Not to tell him we are seeking him, but to see if he is indeed in the Dragon Realm?" Drake had softened his voice.

It didn't help. She crossed her arms over her chest and glared. "Why would I lie to him? We do not lie to one another."

Shows what she knew. I knew she couldn't know about Cian playing footsie with Ailla. My irritation with her lady of the manor nonsense lessened. When she learned the truth, it would devastate her.

"Because you are trying to save him," Taranath said quietly.

Her head whipped towards him, and I swear her eyes nearly bugged out. Snotty she might be, but Dhysara was conflicted about this. I wondered if Cian knew she was pregnant. Something told me he didn't.

Dhysara looked like she might cry. "Do you promise you will not harm him?" She looked right at me when she said it.

"As long as he has nothing to do with the plot against my king," I answered. "If he is not involved, I'll send him home to you."

She studied my face for what seemed a long time. Then she came to her decision. "You may enter, and I shall contact him." She turned and went into the cottage.

"Is this a good idea?" Drake hissed to Taranath, as the two of them fell in behind me.

"She will not harm us if we do not attempt any threatening moves," Taranath said. "The cottage is warded to protect her, so do not try anything that could be interpreted as harm towards the lady. And I have taken over the spell from Iris, so we are protected."

"Noted," Drake said, and it sounded like he was gritting his teeth as he spoke.

Inside, the walls were draped with fabric, making the

small house feel cozy and vibrant all at once. A fireplace at the back had a big fire going in it, and Dhysara went to one of the chairs in front of it. She sat, and pulled something from a basket near the chair. "Sit over there," She pointed at a table across the room. "I do not want him to see you."

We all sat on a bench next to the table.

"I don't like this," Drake whispered.

"I don't either, but if it gets us what we want," I said. I stopped as Dhysara looked at me impatiently. I guess we weren't supposed to talk, either.

She held up a mirror. Did everyone have one? Then I remembered that she was royal, and had lived with a court all her life. So, of course, she would.

"Kelan," she said. The very act of saying her name shot color into her cheeks. She looked like a flower blossoming. "Dearest, are you there?" She cupped the mirror in both hands.

She really loved the crazy asshole. The emotion that I could see on her wasn't fake.

"Sara," a deep voice came from the mirror. "Is all well?"

She nodded as she said, "Of course it is."

"Then why do you call me?"

Wow, what a jerk. How could she not hear the nasty tone he used? Jeez.

"I am wondering when you will return. I miss you, my love."

Oh, God.

My guilt spiked hard. I shoved it back down equally hard. I didn't want to deal with it, and I didn't want her to know I felt it.

"I will return when it is safe to do so. As I told you, I fear my enemies may find me. And you," he added, although that last bit was clearly an afterthought.

He was a total jerk. How did he get this woman to fall in love with him? Devotion to him aside, she seemed sweet.

Dhysara brushed her fingers lightly against the mirror. "I am well, Kelan. I am also very capable of protecting myself." Her hand not holding the mirror skimmed her middle.

He didn't know. Or if he did, he was an even bigger jerk than I thought. He didn't ask about it at all.

"I know you are, Sara." His voice changed.

It sounded to me like some guy on TV selling cars, but Dhysara perked up, and color bloomed in her cheeks.

"Come home soon," she said quietly.

I could hear the longing in her words.

"When the Goblin King has stopped his persecution, I will be able to," Cian said.

Dhysara didn't say anything, and as the silence stretched on, I guessed he'd gone. She stared at the mirror. Then she pulled her shoulders back and stood tall.

"He is in the Dragon Realm. I recognize the castle. But—" She stopped.

Drake had stepped around me, and his right hand rested on his sword.

Dhysara backed up, fear plain across her face. The glow from speaking with Cian faded as though it had never been there. The proud woman who'd met us at the door was gone.

"You swore not to hurt me!" she cried. "It seems I am to die like my father before me!" She raised her hands, to what, I wasn't sure.

"Stop it, both of you," I couldn't keep the irritation out of my voice. Save me from these fae and their drama. "No one is hurting anyone. I'd be happy to discuss the facts of what happened with your father later, as would, I am sure," I gave Drake the sit-down-and-shut-up-hairy eyeball, "the Goblin King. Probably even the Fae King, so that you would have all the knowledge available. But that is not the concern at the moment. No matter what we say here, it won't change what has happened. We need to find Kelan—" I forced myself not to call the jerk Cian— "so that this can get sorted out, and you can have him home." I smiled in what I hoped was a reassuring manner. All this lying didn't come easily to me.

She stared at me, studied me in fact. She wasn't sure if she could believe me, but boy, she wanted to.

"Will you promise not to harm him?"

Hadn't we covered this already? "I cannot promise you that, Lady Dhysara," I said before either Drake or Taranath could put their oars in and muddy things up. "What I can promise you is that he will not be hurt if he is innocent of plotting against the king. But if he lashes out at us, we have no choice to defend ourselves."

She crossed her arms. "You don't help your case, human."

I decided that she wasn't really trying to piss me off. She was just one of those people—fae—who are ingrained with prejudice about those they felt were inferior.

That didn't make me feel any better, but I had to try, dammit.

"I'm being honest. I've never found that honesty hurt my case." I tried to sound light and unaffected. It was not easy when I wanted to slap the smugness out of her.

I kept eye contact with her, not moving. Finally, she sighed and looked down.

"I can give you the location of where it seems he is. I am not sure, and I want that clear, so if he is not there, it is not held against me."

"Fine," I said. "Show us on a map," and I felt Taranath rustling in his pack next to me. I wanted to turn and look at him, but I also didn't want to look away from her. She was so suspicious and ready to take offense that it felt like I needed to walk on eggshells. But I could also sense a desperation in her, and I chalked it up to being pregnant. And growing up in loony tunesville. It gave me a glimpse of why all the kids who'd grown up in the Dragon Realm were such problems now. Eilor was a nut, and he'd raised Ailla, Cian, and Dhysara in that environment. I filed that away for consideration later.

Taranath walked beyond her to a table and unrolled a map. "If you would, please, Lady Dhysara."

His quiet tone and respectful manner seemed to calm her. She stood near him, and I stood next to her. I felt like Drake looming over her would destroy the tiny bit of whatever good we'd managed.

"Here," she said, pointing at a place on the map that I couldn't read. I had to get around to learning Fae. Maybe when I got my husband back and wasn't living in a state of crisis.

"This is where we have gone to spend time together. It's one of Eilor's personal estates, not any part of the Dragon Realm holdings. It's very private." She didn't look at any of us.

"Thank you, Lady Dhysara," Taranath said, rolling

up the map. He turned, putting it back into the pack as he did so. I watched him over my shoulder, and then Drake moved to join him. I made to follow when Dhysara's hand shot out and grabbed my wrist.

I didn't see anything but the intensity of her eyes, although I heard the hiss of Drake's sword leaving the scabbard.

"It's okay," I said, not looking away. God, I hope it's okay. I'll never hear the end of it if I'm wrong.

"Please try to keep him safe," she said. "He is sometimes...fierce in his opinions."

That was the understatement of the year, if not the century. He was insane, but I couldn't say that to her.

"I can only work with what he gives us," I said, wanting to be honest.

She squeezed my hand. "That is the best I can hope for. This has been coming for a long time." She dropped her hand from mine and turned away from all of us. "Please leave now. I want no one to see you here."

Who would see anything? I wanted to ask, but I didn't. "Thank you, Lady Dhysara," I said, backing towards the door.

She crossed her arms, and I saw her head nod a bit, but she didn't speak or turn around.

In spite of the roller coaster of emotions being around her brought, I was left with pity for her. She had what I termed Dragon Realm Crazy all over her, but...did she ever really have a choice? Or maybe I felt bad for her being pregnant with Cian. I didn't know. I couldn't hate her. I certainly didn't feel the same level of animosity I felt for Cian and Ailla.

I let Drake and Taranath leave, and then I backed out of the door, closing it behind me. It seemed important that I didn't turn my back on her, no matter how much pity I felt. I wasn't thrilled at my gut warning about that, but whatever. We were out of there, and as I turned, Drake was bringing my horse to me.

Without words, we all mounted and then rode in silence. None of us wanted to speak until we were safely away.

8

Iris

"We have a problem," Drake announced after we'd been riding for a while.

"Only one?" I felt my eyebrows raise.

"We need to stop and let me get a look at the map," Drake reined his horse and moved over to the side of the path we were on.

Taranath and I did the same, and I slid down from the horse. Drake was already unrolling the map.

"Look," Drake said, and I could hear something— anger?—in his tone. "This is the castle that the woman indicated. Look how far into the Dragon Realm it is."

I peered more closely at it. It didn't look that far, but Taranath was nodding.

"It will take us some time to reach this place on horse," he said.

"Really? But it doesn't look that far," I said before I could stop myself.

"Ladyship, allow for the fact that I might know the land," Drake snapped.

"Ease up, Mr. Intensity! It doesn't look that far on the map. Perhaps the fae need some work on their mapmaking skills!"

"What would you know about maps?"

"Oh, I don't know! Maybe that I looked at them every day for years? And they were accurate regarding representing a realistic distance!" I yelled back.

"This is not helping us solve our problem," Taranath said, taking the map from Drake. "There is only one solution, my lord. And—"

"I know, I know!" Drake threw up his hands. "We have to portal."

"But—" I felt lost all of a sudden. Wasn't the point of bruising my ass that we couldn't portal? "I thought we couldn't because we'd be spotted and all that?"

Taranath nodded. "We will be. If not by Cian and his associates, by someone else. It will not allow for us to move about quietly. But Drake is right. We will spend too much time trying to get to the castle that Dhysara indicated."

I held up a hand, and he stopped, looking at me expectantly. "I know this is a little off-topic, but I have to ask. I felt sorry for Dhysara," I kept the theory about her upbringing to myself for the moment, "But there was something creepy as hell about her, wasn't there?"

That made Drake smile a little. "You mean other than her choice of a mate?"

"She really loves him, but..." I thought about it. "She is obsessed."

"That can be dangerous," Taranath said. "She does seem extremely focused on him."

"She's pregnant," I said.

"What?" Drake said.

Taranath nodded again. "I noticed that as well, my lady."

"She didn't look pregnant," Drake protested.

"She totally is," I said. "You couldn't see her cradling her stomach? She wants him home. I think that's the only reason she was cooperative with us at all."

"This is not good," Drake said, turning away and beginning to pace in frustration. "What do you know about fae children, Iris?"

"I know that there aren't that many."

He nodded. "It's considered a good sign for the

marriage when a child is created. And to know that this will potentially turn into a twisted child like Cian —the mind boggles at the thought. Even once we rid ourselves of Cian, there's another little—"

"No! You're not thinking about—" I couldn't even say the words.

"It would depend on how the child was raised. Look at the king and Cian," Taranath said. "The same parents, but one child is a good man and good ruler, and the other is—"

"Insane," I finished. "And Dhysara doesn't seem to have the best grasp of reality, plus, she has a massive ego," I remembered her snotty comments about the usurper. "That doesn't bode well for her child-raising skills."

"She also has the mistaken impression that she should have been the next in line for the Goblin Throne. Who knows what assumptions she would pass onto a child?" Taranath sounded bothered, and that was saying something.

He never seemed bothered. That scared me.

"We are not considering hurting her or the baby!" I couldn't believe we were speaking of this.

Taranath shook his head and patted my hand. "No, your Majesty, we are not. We are not monsters, even though this creates problems for the King and yourself. No, we are assessing the potential problems. It is something that will have to be dealt with."

"I don't like the way that sounds—'something to be dealt with'," I said. "I can't support that. We have to find a solution that doesn't involve violence against an innocent kid!"

Drake rolled his eyes, but Taranath smiled. "We will, your Majesty. We are not unkind, or cruel. But preparation with knowledge of challenges makes ruling far easier than reacting as something is occurring."

"Well, we have time to consider the issues of a little Cian," Drake interrupted. "Stay focused, please. We need to decide how we're going to manage this distance." He pointed at the map that Taranath still held.

"Of course we're going to portal," Taranath said. "However, the question is how to conceal ourselves, such as we can."

"Any ideas are welcome," Drake said dryly.

I kept quiet. I had found that even though Taranath got to where he wanted to go slowly, it paid off to let him take his time. He was careful and thoughtful, and usually right.

"We have Iris direct the portal," he said.

"No!" Drake and I said together.

"I'm not that good at it. Not even a little bit good," I protested.

"Who knows where we'll end up, even if we do make it?" Drake asked at the same time.

"Thanks for the vote of confidence," I snarled at Drake.

"Just being honest, ladyship," Drake shot back. "You know, that thing you prize so highly?"

I had to walk away. The urge to slap him was strong. It didn't help that he was right. Portal travel made me nervous. I didn't have a good idea of how it was supposed to go because most of my portal travel had been affected by the spell that Ailla put on me. Even now, the thought of it made my stomach roll around uneasily. I knew this was because I still struggled with the after effects of the spell and that it didn't have jack to do with actual portal travel, but my mind couldn't get past it. One more reason I got first dibs on Ailla.

I stood with my back to the others, breathing deeply. We were all stressed, and the meeting with Dhysara was lingering in the creepy column. I'd made it through stress before, but worry over Brennan, worry that we'd be too late, and the fact that I knew I was out of my element with a lot of this made it worse for me. I felt pretty sure Drake was seething with anger, and anger didn't make good decisions.

Neither did fear, and I had to stop worrying about what I didn't know. I was with two people who, snark from Drake aside, would be at my side no matter what. Taranath thought I was doing well. Although...I turned back.

"Why is it exactly that you want me to do the portal?" I asked.

"Because he has decided he has a death wish," muttered Drake.

Taranath didn't even let on that he'd heard Drake. "Because your magic is not anything that is known to the practitioners who might be monitoring what is going on," he said with a smile. "You're an unknown quantity. The Fae King cut your celebration short, remember? No one knows you, other than you're a human who has survived the transition to the Fae Realm. They will not know of your skills. No one does."

"Other than the goblins," I said, remembering them humming The Bridal March and feeling my eyes fill with tears. They were loyal, but Cian had somehow gotten a healthy number to attack both Brennan and Drake right before we met. There had to be a spy or someone who wasn't loyal somewhere. And those in the castle were everywhere. They knew everything.

"Oh, I put a silencing spell on the castle staff. They will not be able to speak of you, or anything they know of you, or that the King is missing. I also think that the Fae King will do his best to pretend that our King is still there."

"But I'm not, and they have to notice that." Hmm. A silencing spell? That was convenient. "That was thinking ahead," I added.

Taranath nodded, accepting the compliment.

"People, even goblins, see what they expect to," Drake said. "Although I agree that there is still a mystery in regards to how Cian was able to get goblins from our Realm to attack us. But Taranath is right—we didn't leave exposure from those at the castle to chance." He heaved a great sigh. "I hate to admit it, but Taranath is right about you, too. Even though it might kill us all. No one is expecting to see your magic."

"What does that mean?" I asked impatiently. "How can people see magic? You're not making sense!" I was also stalling. I didn't want to do the portal.

Taranath gave me a look that said he knew what I was up to but I didn't care. "Everyone who does magic has a..." he thought for a moment, "A signature if you will. Rather like signing your name—everyone's is different, you see?"

I nodded.

He continued, "And there are people throughout the Realms who monitor the magic they sense in their Realm as well as their neighbors. I can guarantee that his Majesty is monitored. As much as he can be," he added cryptically.

"Why has no one else noticed Cian and his drop in visits?" I interrupted.

Taranath shrugged. "I do not have an answer, although I suspect he works to mask his magic. After all, we hadn't felt him in the castle other than when he showed up in the flames in the courtyard. So he is skilled at hiding himself when he wants to."

"Which is why it's a good thing to have you do this, although I fear for us all," Drake said, and he gave me a smile that contained an apology.

I couldn't help it and smiled back. He was a pain in the ass, but he was loyal, and I knew I could trust him. He wasn't saying anything I didn't think. He was just more of a jerk about it.

"All right," I sighed. "I guess I'll have to be the one to do it. I need help, though." I looked at the two of them.

"As if we'd do anything else," Drake snorted. "I want to live, after all."

The time to be nice was apparently over.

"What do we do with the horses?" I asked. I knew I was dawdling. I could feel my heart beat faster.

"I shall attend to that," Taranath bowed his head and stepped away. He pulled a mirror from somewhere and began to speak into it.

"Stop stalling," Drake said to me quietly. "You have to do this. And in all honesty, Iris, you can do this. You are more skilled than you realize. You need to visualize it, and you'll manage the portal."

"But I have no idea what this place looks like!" I could feel my heart rise to the top of my chest. It threatened to choke me, and I felt like I wanted to take a lot of deep breaths.

He pulled the map out once more. "That makes it a little more challenging, but it's not even close to impossible before you try and protest again. Here, look at the place on the map."

He held it out while I stared at it.

"Now close your eyes, and imagine the map in your mind. See it, and if you're not sure, look at the map again."

Taranath rejoined us, tucking his mirror away. He'd also taken a large pack from his horse. I had mine strapped to me, and Drake seemed to travel with all his belongings attached to his body. So I guessed that we were going to do this, right now. I didn't see any other way to delay.

I noticed that Drake and Taranath were watching me carefully, and continued to do so as I looked at the map a few more times.

"Can you see it?" Drake asked.

I nodded.

"Then here, take this," he put a stone into my hand. "Focus on the stone, and having the stone take you to the place on the map."

Okay, you can do this, I told myself. I took a couple more deep breaths, focusing on the picture of the map in my head. I thought, Take us there! I felt the stone in my hand warm, and I focused on the map again.

The stone got hotter. I held it more tightly, forcing everything from my head but the picture of the map.

A whoosh, like the air had been sucked from me, and then I felt the ripples, although mine didn't feel as smooth as Brennan's. The daylight from where we'd stopped the horses disappeared and the air got cooler.

Well, we'd definitely portaled somewhere. I opened my eyes, and we were in a cave. Or maybe the dungeons? I glanced to my side and saw that Drake and Taranath were next to me.

"Where are we?" I asked, taking a step forward.

And fell flat on my face.

9

Brennan

He kept his eyes closed as the door opened. The way it slammed, he knew it wasn't his mysterious benefactor from before. Whoever this was made no effort to hide.

"Might as well give it up," Cian's mocking tones said near his head. "I know you're not sleeping."

"I was hoping that if you thought I was, you'd leave," Brennan said, opening his eyes to meet those of his brother's.

A flash of something—anger, perhaps—crossed Cian's face quickly. It left just as quickly as it had come. His brother still had the easily stirred temper he'd had as a child. It would be funny if it weren't sad. All this time and Cian had not evolved. He'd been right, in his musing earlier.

Why?

"Where have you been all this time?" He asked, hoping to find out something—anything—that might help him. He was also curious. How had Cian escaped detection by everyone for over six hundred years? He'd been well hidden all this time. Who would have the nerve to lie to Fae King in this manner?

Cian laughed, and it was like hearing an old man cackle. "Wouldn't you like to know?"

"Yes, I would," Brennan said, taking on his tone that he used for those who came to him to complain and have justice meted out. "Father and Mother would have welcomed you home. And they truly believed you'd died in a fire."

Cian looked at him for a moment, then said, "I set the fire. I wanted them to think me dead."

Brennan shook his head before he could stop himself, mystified. "Why? They loved you greatly, Cian, as did I."

Cian got close, leaning down so that Brennan could see the madness in his eyes. "No, you didn't. You never did. You were merely waiting for the time to push me aside. And when it came, that is exactly what you did!" Spittle formed one corner of his mouth.

Brennan found this aspect of Cian alarming. Well,

there were a number of disturbing aspects, but this was one of the most. His brother truly believed that he'd been pushed aside. Brennan couldn't decide whether Cian was more angry or determined to be a persecuted being. He vacillated between the two.

Might as well see which one his brother identified with more. "No, I was waiting for nothing. And Mother and Father were never the same after you left."

"Well, why would they be? They'd gotten rid of me, and were happy to focus on you, the precious heir to the Goblin Throne!"

Brennan couldn't tell if Cian knew the importance of being the Goblin King, the responsibility he held in partnership with the Fae King for the entire Realm. He realized that he would never have been able to work with Cian as he worked with his father. The Realms would have fallen into disarray at best, if not civil war.

"No, I don't think so. Father was not happy when he told me I'd been chosen." Brennan remembered that well. It had hurt to think his father was disappointed, which is what Brennan thought at the time. He'd waited until Brennan was about to take the Goblin Throne before he'd told him the truth—Brennan hoped with all he had that his father had never told Cian. "Nor was I. I liked the Goblin King, and I liked Dhysara." He watched carefully to see what Cian did when he mentioned his wife's name.

Only the lowering of brows showed that Cian wasn't pleased Brennan remembered or knew of her. "Dhysara is as sweet as she is stupid. And even she is too good for you. You who stole her inheritance!"

"Dhysara was not slated to rule the Goblin Realm," Brennan said calmly. "I met with the Goblin King. He knew that his line would not rule after him."

"Because Father decided that his precious, useless son needed somewhere to land!" Cian spat. "He also knew that I would never tolerate you taking things not yours, so he got rid of me. He let you hurt me! You could have killed me, and Father did nothing! He didn't send you away! He sent me! Not you!"

Fast as a lightning strike, Cian punched Brennan in the face. It was unexpected, and Brennan's head jerked sideways from the impact. He could feel blood leaking down his lip. With his hands bound, he couldn't even rub his face. He turned back and looked at Cian coldly.

"How mature, Cian. To use fists to express anger." He knew he was pushing Cian, but he didn't care. Not at the moment.

"Oh, I shall express my anger, as you put it, magically as well. That is coming. Don't worry on that account," Cian said, a smile on his face. Hitting Brennan seemed to have released the anger within.

For the moment.

"You still have not answered my earlier question. Where have you been all this time? With Dhysara?"

It bothered Cian that Brennan knew of her. A thing to note. He'd have to use her name whenever possible. Because an angry Cian made poor decisions. And poor decisions might offer him an opportunity for escape.

It also meant he'd probably visited more pain on himself, but if it meant he might have more of a chance, it was worth the pain.

"Or is she merely your latest hiding place?" He put a hint of scorn in the question, to see if Cian might catch it.

Cian's face reddened, but he sounded composed when he answered. "Why all the questions, brother? Why do you care now?"

"I am merely curious who would have kept the son of the Fae King hidden all these years."

Cian laughed. "You are so naïve, Brennan! As though using Father or his supposed importance as something to fear has any effect on people living outside the Fae Court."

"It doesn't?" Brennan struggled with where the conversation was heading. There had been a shift, one that he couldn't follow.

Cian was mad. What had happened to him? Fae didn't normally go mad like this.

Cian came around so that Brennan could see him fully. "You really want to know, little brother? I shall tell you, and then you will know how people really feel about Father and you." He laughed, but turned away, crossing his arms.

He doesn't believe what he's saying to me, Brennan thought. But he kept quiet, wanting to hear what Cian would say.

"When you tried to kill me, I didn't die. But I did fall into a sleep, and I didn't wake from it until I'd been moved to the castle with Margot."

Margot? Brennan racked his brain. Who was Margot? He thought back through childhood. She was —she was their nanny. Well, she was supposed to be the nanny to him and Cian, but she'd always favored Cian. It made sense that Margot had been sent with him.

"When I woke, I knew that I wasn't at our home. In my rooms, in my castle. So I pretended to be unknowing, to see what those around me would tell me. And do you know what Margot said?" He turned back to Brennan, his eyes slanting at he smiled.

"I have no idea," Brennan answered.

"She told me that my parents were horrible, and had sent me away because they favored my brother. My younger brother. That they had given that brother all that was mine, but that she loved me, and she would not only take care of me but make sure I got the things I deserved, the things that were stolen from me."

He laughed, but it was not a happy laugh. "Margot might have been a bit biased, but she wasn't wrong. They did favor you. Why they made such a fuss when you were declared the heir to the Goblin Throne—stealing Dhysara's inheritance as well—I shall never know. But it doesn't matter. Our parents made their choice, and now, finally, they will pay for it."

"You're wrong. They mourned you every day. They mourn your loss still," Brennan said, thinking about the fact that he and Nerida weren't speaking because of it. Nerida wasn't talking to any of her family because of her continued mourning.

Cian wasn't listening. He was tapping his finger on his chin, thinking. "You know, it's interesting, Brennan. You stole from me when you turned our parents against me. Then you stole from Dhysara. How fitting it is that we shall take back all that you stole. Once I have finished with you, I will be the ruler of the Goblin Realm and the Fae King, and you, you will be nothing. As you deserve to be."

Had this not been absurd, Brennan would have laughed out loud. The thought that this man—he couldn't think of him as a brother any longer—felt he could manage both Realms, and felt that he was entitled to do so was funny. In a dark, twisted way, as Cian would ruin both, but funny nonetheless.

If he could ignore the horrifying idea of Cian running his realm, not to mention being around Iris. What would happen to Iris? He found that he had to put his worry for her into a separate space. Otherwise, it would take over all his thoughts, to his detriment. This was not the time to let his guard down, not even a little.

"That's all very nice to ponder," Brennan drawled, "But it hasn't happened yet, has it? How many times is it you've attempted to rid yourself of me? Three? Four? You're not making a good showing, Cian."

Cian flicked his hand, and Brennan found himself unable to move and racked with pain. His jaw clenched shut. He could feel his teeth grinding together.

"Not very smart, are you little brother? You're not in a position to negotiate, bargain, or do much of anything. You continue to talk as though you are. You are nothing, Brennan. You've always been nothing. Once I'm done with you, all will see you for what you really are. Then I can turn my attention to making the Realms as they should be."

The last thought Brennan had before he passed out was that at least he wasn't being drained.

Iris

*J*erked in fear. I felt—I didn't know what I felt, but it hurt. My whole being hurt. I wanted to curl up and scream out loud.

But why? I'd fallen, yes. But falling onto the rough ground wasn't enough to feel this kind of pain.

"Your Majesty, let me help you." Taranath's voice said above me.

I felt his hand reach for mine, and partially lift me as I got to my feet.

"Is this the castle?" I asked, hearing the breathlessness in my voice. Pain will do that to you. Another wave hit, and I leaned over, putting my hands on my legs.

"What's wrong?" Drake asked.

I held up a hand, trying to breathe through the pain. It finally ebbed, and I stood up, feeling sweat on my face. "I must have hit hard because wow, that hurt to get up."

Taranath came into view, holding a light of some sort. I didn't realize how dark this place was. "What do you mean it hurt to get up?"

"It felt like I hit a major nerve or something when I fell because I hurt all over."

"Have you experienced this before?"

I shook my head, forgetting we were mostly in the dark. "No. This is new and weird, like lots of things in this world."

"This is not pain from falling. It's some manner of magical pain," Taranath said with surety. "I cannot tell what is causing it because there is no significant surge of magic here, or really, wards of any kind. But that was not a result of your fall."

"Nice job, by the way," Drake quipped. "So nice to land in this pest hole, wherever it is."

"Shut up," I said. "Aren't you supposed to try and be helpful? How about finding out if we're in the castle we're aiming for?" I rubbed my head. The pain had passed, but I still had that feeling you have when you've had to make it through something horrible. It was relief mixed with memory, and the memory sucked.

"Had you not landed us in the cave of wherever, we might have an idea," Drake shot back.

Some empathy this guy had. At that moment, Taranath intervened.

"I can't tell what just happened, your Majesty, but if you can walk comfortably, let us move forward and see if we can determine where we are."

He sounded fake-hopeful, and that made me feel even worse. First time driving, and I drop us in a hole somewhere.

Taranath held his light—a torch of some kind—high. I could see a little more, and it looked like a cave. Weren't castles built on caves? Isn't that where dungeons came from? I hoped so.

We walked on, Drake in the rear and mumbling. He was speaking in Fae and sounded grumpy as hell.

"That is not helpful, my lord," said Taranath.

Yep. Grumpy as hell. Probably complaining, too.

"I have to let it out," Drake said. "Isn't that your mantra, ladyship? Be honest, get things out in the open? I am putting my disappointment and frustration out in the open."

"How in the hell does Brennan stand you? You don't have an off button ever, do you?" I whirled around, annoyed. Jeez, I was just learning all this shit. "I'm not a thousand years old with loads of experience like yourself! You think you could cut me a little slack? You know, because that's what people do when others are learning? And aren't we supposed to be friends? Is this how you treat your friends? No wonder you don't have any!"

I clapped my hand over my mouth to stop anything further from coming out. I knew me. I would go from here to digging at him about Ailla, and that wasn't nice, or fair. I just hated feeling like a failure, and not having someone try and help me move past it. Most of the people in my life didn't rub it in.

"This is not a game, your Majesty," Drake said, and I could hear the real anger in his words. "If we do not get to where we need to be, your husband, my king, my brother—will die. It's that simple. I don't appreciate being tossed about to and fro when we need you to concentrate—"

"Drake," Taranath said. He sounded angry.

"What?"

"You are being unkind, and extremely unhelpful. No one is perfect in the craft of magic. You know this. Iris is doing extremely well. You know this also."

Silence greeted his words. Taranath didn't yell at anyone, ever. This stern rebuke was the same as me pitching a fit. I didn't feel sorry for Drake, though. Taking his shit out on me only made things worse.

"Regardless, I believe I can answer the question of where we are," Taranath said in a more normal tone.

"How?" Drake and I asked together.

"There's a door." The light bobbed in front of us to the left.

I followed the motion and could see the faint outline of the door.

"Good," Drake sounded gruff. "Taranath, I will open it. You be ready to stop anyone that comes through. I'll be right next to you," He drew his sword. "You," He turned to me, "Stay behind us. Taranath is right, you're doing okay with your skills, but you are not anywhere near ready for a battle. Stay behind us. Do you understand?"

There was an apology there. I could hear it, although he'd never say the words out loud. Which meant I needed to do the same.

"I do. I won't get in the way," I said.

A moment, and then he nodded at me. I knew that this was forgiven, on both sides. We were both worried, and apparently had the same sort of temper. With something that I thought might be hysteria, I made another mental tick in the 'just alike' column for Drake and I. Brennan had married the girl Drake. I stopped myself at the thought of Brennan. I couldn't afford to get all bananas. Nor did I want to think about how I wasn't bothered at all that I was just like Brennan's other favorite person. In contrast, the thought made me feel warm.

Brennan. Please be safe; please be alive, I thought. Drake was right. We were on a ticking clock. I only hoped we'd get to him in time.

Drake moved quietly to the door. Taranath stood to the side, ready for...what? I couldn't tell what he was doing as he'd moved the light to up above him—how was he making it float like that?—and dimmed it.

That was a trick I needed to learn, stat.

Drake pulled the door open quickly, leaping backward as he did so.

With a yell, they were practically on top of us.

10

——————

Iris

*D*rake yelled something in Fae, and I felt my heart try to burst out of my chest. I didn't know what to do because anything I did might not be helpful.

Taranath stepped closer, and I could see a blue flame shooting from his hands. Whatever it was caused damage; there was yelping from the horde of whatever had come through the door.

I took a couple of steps back trying to figure out exactly what it was that had come through the door. They were bigger, and...I covered my nose. Wow, did they smell. What the hell was that? It smelled like something had died.

"Ewww," I said, not able to stop myself.

"Iris!" Taranath yelled. "Time to try again!" He didn't look at me, focusing on whatever he was shooting from his hands towards the stinky guys.

I stared, not sure what he—Oh! Time to portal again. Oh, God. Because I'd done so well before. It had to be better than these smelly giants trying to kill us. I hoped, anyway. I felt in my pockets. I didn't have a stone! Shit! How was I supposed to steer without one? I could feel the panic rise as Drake and one of the smellies landed close to me with a thud.

I jumped back and then closed my eyes, taking deep breaths.

"Concentrate, you can do this," I muttered. I pictured Drake, Taranath and me at the place on the map that I could see in my head. "Take us there," I said, not sure who I spoke to.

My fists were clenched and I could feel something...sort of like ripples. "To the castle, to the castle, me, Drake, and Taranath, to the castle," I said.

The ripples increased. The smelly giants were yelling, in a language I couldn't understand, and I opened my eyes.

Taranath was next to me, although he was still sending the blue flame to the whatevers that had burst in the door.

All of a sudden, his flame died, and I could see one of the giants heading right for us.

"Iris!" Drake yelled.

Then he threw himself in front of Taranath and I. Taranath grabbed my hand.

"Now, please," he said, sounding like we were talking about the weather and not about to die.

I squeezed my eyes shut and thought about the castle on the map.

The ripples grabbed me, and it went silent. The silence seemed louder for the noise that we'd just left. The castle, the castle, the castle, I thought. Please get us there.

I could tell that we'd landed somewhere, but where? I didn't want to open my eyes.

"What were you thinking about when you directed the portal, your Majesty?" Taranath asked from beside me.

I was back to being the queen again. I noticed when stress levels were high, they both called me Iris, but I didn't mind. I didn't open my eyes yet. "I kept thinking, get us to the castle, and picturing the place on the map," I said.

"Well, we're at a castle, of sorts." Drake sounded amused.

Which was better than mad.

I opened my eyes. "Where are we? Where were we? What the hell were those huge smelly guys?"

Taranath laughed. "Those were trolls, part of the guard if I had to guess. They do carry a distinctive odor about them. It's part of their culture. I believe they find it appealing."

"Oh, Lord. Really?" I couldn't come up with anything that wasn't hugely insulting.

"They do smell. But should a visit be necessary, you get used to it," Drake laughed as well. "Which leads me to believe you sent us to the Troll Realm."

"I thought we were friends! Why did they attack us?"

"I would have done the same," Drake shrugged, and oddly, put his sword back into the scabbard. "We weren't supposed to be there, and they didn't know who we were. I'll have Brenn—" He stopped.

My heart fell. But if I let it keep falling, I'd be no good to anyone. I straightened my shoulders. "One of us will contact them once this is over," I finished his thought with more conviction than I felt, "And explain...well, I don't know what, but we'll come up with something. So where are we?"

Taranath had been looking around while Drake and I talked. Now he turned his gaze on me. "Were you panicked when you opened the portal?" He asked.

I nodded. "Well, yes. All I could see was you, and your flashy hands and Drake and lots of giants headed right for me."

"That explains it, then. You brought us to where you feel safe."

"What does that mean? I don't feel safe anywhere."

"It means you've brought us back to the Human Realm," Taranath said.

"I believe this is what is called 'taking the long way' to get somewhere, isn't it?" Drake asked.

I looked around. "I have no idea where we are, although this does kind of look like a castle. A little one."

Taranath looked like he was holding back a smile. I didn't see the humor in this. Wasn't Drake just screaming about how being late would kill Brennan? What the hell?

"You're getting better," Drake said. "At least you got one part right. That's better than a cave in the Troll Realm."

He and Taranath looked at one another, and both started to laugh. I put my hands on my hips. "What is going on? We're wasting time! Isn't that what you were just saying? Or is it we still have enough time to make fun of Iris?"

Drake laughed harder, although Taranath calmed down. He watched Drake for a moment, then turned to me. "Your learning curve, I believe that's what you call it, is funny, your Majesty. But you are getting better. How do you feel?"

"Mad, and tired," I said.

"As you should. Two portals in such a short amount of time are wearing on anyone, especially one just learning."

"Is that supposed to make me feel better? Because this one," I gestured at Drake, "Is ruining it."

Drake stood up, his laughter dying. "I am sorry, but Taranath is right. You'll laugh at this at a later date, ladyship."

"I think you're cracking under stress, and you—" I stopped as I saw Drake draw his sword and place himself in front of me. Taranath moved behind me, and I could feel his back as he faced away from me.

I don't know when they managed it, but three men had come up and surrounded us. They were crouched low, almost like animals. The tension was so heavy I could cut it with a knife.

"You wanna tell me how you just dropped into my front yard?" The words were quiet, but even I could hear the menace in them. "You have about sixty seconds."

I looked at the man who spoke. He was young, although he was older than me. His arms were crossed, and he had dark hair and dark eyes that suggested we'd better answer fast.

Although I thought Drake could take him. But the other two, who were younger, one blond, one sandy-haired, I wasn't sure. They were itching for a fight. All it would take was the speaker to say the word, and they'd be on us like white on rice.

I held up a hand, for both Drake and the two young guys, and took one step towards Crossed Arms. "My name is Iris, and I am here by mistake. But speaking of that, can you tell me where here is?"

Whatever he'd expected, that wasn't it. I could tell by the lone eyebrow that raised.

"Where do you think you are?"

Oh, he was crafty. But I didn't have time for this macho back-and-forth who has more info dance. "I think we're in the Human Realm—I mean, I think we're on Earth. Beyond that, I don't know. I'm from Florida, and this looks nothing like it."

"What do you mean, the Human Realm?" The blonde guy asked.

Shit. I didn't mean to say that, but it had slipped out. "It's nothing. Just the way we speak, so if you could —" I stopped as Crossed Arms took a step towards me, causing Drake to stick his sword in between us.

Crossed Arms gave Drake the side eye, and with

one hand, pushed the sword away. He leaned in closer and sniffed.

Okay, what the hell?

"What are you?" He asked. He leaned towards Drake and sniffed again. "You're not the same as she is —what are you?"

Now it was my turn to be surprised. "Uh, we're like you, only dressed differently," I started. Well, I wasn't. I was still sporting my jeans and sweater. But Drake and Taranath looked...off. The long coat/robes probably didn't help.

"Uh, uh. You may look human, and you're part human, but this is something more. I can smell it."

"What are you, a dog?" Drake asked contemptuously.

Only a growl—a growl!—from Crossed Arms stopped the other two from leaping on Drake. He wasn't bothered at all.

"What, that offend you, little boys? Come on; I'm ready!" Drake swung his sword, crouching low as they had before.

I'd never understood what 'the light of battle in their eyes' meant, but I did now. I was surrounded by the fight club and they were all raring to go.

"Stop!" I shouted. Everyone turned to look at me. I didn't figure we were supposed to blow our cover, but if this guy was sniffing things out, what the hell? He wasn't normal either.

"You're right. We're not human. I'm part human, part fae. My companions, Drake and Taranath, are both fae. We're here—I'd love it if you would tell me where here is, as I asked earlier—because I took a wrong turn. If you could just forget you saw us, we'll get out of your way."

"Nope," said Crossed Arms. "Not how it works. You're some otherworldly type—you should know better than to just land into the territory of others without letting them know."

"We're kind of on the type of journey where we'd rather people not know," I snapped. "What is your name, by the way? I'm Iris." I held out a hand.

He looked at me, and then my hand, and back at me as he slowly reached out and shook it. He had a firm grip, and I could feel some unyielding power, almost like an electric force, running through him. That must be the fae in me because I'd never noticed that about people before.

"I'm Max."

"Where are we?"

"Idaho Springs."

"Which is in what state?" I asked. God, this was painful!

"Colorado. Where is the fae territory?"

"What are you and how did you know we were here?"

"We're shifters, and I saw you drop into the front yard. Where do the fae claim?"

"We are not from your world," Taranath finally spoke. "There are worlds other than the human one, and that is where the fae claim. We are from the Fae Realm. You can only access it via portal travel. As her Majesty said—"

"Her majesty?" Sandy-hair laughed. "She doesn't look majestic at all!" His laugh ended abruptly as Max gave him the shut up look.

"Is that true?" Max asked me.

I wasn't comfortable with my new role or advertising it. But this wasn't a normal human, and I guessed he could handle something that anyone else would toss me into an asylum over. "Yes. I married the King of the Goblin Realm two days ago—" a sob caught in my throat as I realized it had only been two days! It seemed so much longer! Oh god, we were wasting time!

"She is, in fact, the Goblin Queen. We are in search of someone important in our Realm, and as she is still new to the art of magic, we have not quite made it where we wished to be."

I was so thankful for Taranath's calm interruption.

"Come inside," Max said. "This is probably better

discussed indoors. Kirk," he looked at the blond, "You two do a quick check for anyone else, and get back here."

The other two nodded and took off in a run. Max looked at all three of us. "Come inside," he said again. "The sooner we talk, the sooner you are on your way."

"There is no reason for us to tarry here, Iris," said Drake. "These shifters, whatever they are, have nothing to do with our business."

Max, who had turned, apparently expecting us to follow, stopped, and took four steps so that he stood right in Drake's personal space. "If someone entered your place, would you let them leave without finding out what was going on with them? Or would you invite them in to share your hospitality, and keep your realm safe?" He crossed his arms again, waiting for Drake to answer.

Drake sheathed his sword and rolled his eyes. "You have a point, shifter, but we are in a hurry. So let's move this along so that we may be on our way. Time is not our friend."

Max turned his back and walked into the castle. Once inside, it was a cozy study, with wood-paneled walls and green above the picture rail where various prints resided. It reminded me of an English country castle, or what I thought it should look like.

"Please sit," Max said. As we did so, he asked, "Would you care for a drink?"

"Water, please," I said immediately. Food and drink didn't seem important until I thought about how long it had been since I'd had any.

He stepped to the door of the room, and I heard him speak, but I couldn't understand what he said.

"What are we going to tell him?" I hissed at the other two. "I thought we weren't advertising what was really going on!" I stopped as Max came back.

He sat, and steepled his fingers. He looked a lot older when he did that.

The door burst open, and the sandy-haired guy came in with a tray that had a pitcher of water and some glasses. Kirk followed behind him. Sandy Hair poured each of us a glass, and then Max. Then he went and stood behind Max's chair.

It made me think of a king.

Like my king. I took a deep breath to keep the tears from falling. Dammit, why couldn't I be more like the fae at times like this? I pulled myself together. I'd been outed as a queen; I needed to behave like one. I'd be able to break down and sob later sometime. Next year, maybe.

I looked around, realizing that everyone was staring at me, obviously waiting for me to say something.

"I'm sorry, I was thinking about something else. Did you ask me a question?"

Sandy Hair and Kirk both snickered, and Max's brows gathered together, indicating he wasn't pleased with my answer.

"I did. Who are you looking for, and why do you suspect they are here?"

Jeez. How much to tell, here? I took a deep breath and looked him in the eyes. "We are looking for, as Drake said, someone important to the Realm. It's better to keep the who part of this quiet. We didn't come here on purpose. I am not all that skilled at portal travel—that's how we travel—" I saw Kirk roll his eyes but continued, "And since I am from the Human Realm, I must have steered us here by accident."

Then I waited.

"This person you're looking for," Max said finally, "Man or woman?"

"Man," I said promptly.

"Does he travel alone?"

That wasn't what I expected, and it must have struck Drake as odd, too.

"Why do you ask?" He interrupted.

Sandy Hair started to speak when Max held up his hand. Sandy Hair stopped as quickly as he'd begun.

"Our companion probably would not be alone,"

Taranath said, "But as he is with the people he's with under duress, I doubt he'd be moving about freely."

"What have you seen?" Drake asked.

I could hear the rising anger in his voice. I wondered if the shifters could—yep, they could. The two behind Max tensed. I put a hand on his arm, trying to tell him to shut the hell up with the attitude. With a pretty please. While I'd landed us here by mistake, it sounded like Max might have some information that could help us.

Unless I was wrong about why he was all cagey.

"Three days ago, we picked up the scent of those who smell like you," Max pointed at Taranath and Drake. "It is not one we're familiar with, and as you might have noticed, we take visitors to our territory seriously. We followed them into the town. They moved as though they were totally unaware of those around them."

"Almost like everyone else was invisible," Kirk added.

Max nodded. "They were strange. We didn't get close to them because unlike you, they didn't land in my front yard," he smiled, and I could see more of the normal guy versus the scary shifter guy. "Then they disappeared, and although the scent was still around, I had no idea where they went to."

"Why would anyone be in the Human Realm?" I asked Taranath.

"What did they look like? How many were there?" Drake asked.

"A man and a woman. The man was tall, with a large scar—" Max stopped as Drake jumped up.

Kirk and Sandy Hair—I needed to ask this dude's name—jumped in front of Max into crouches so fast I didn't even see them move.

_____

11

Brennan

*H*e closed his eyes, trying to move beyond the pain. It worked, for a few moments and then without warning, a wave of pain rolled through his body. It was bad enough that Cian hurt him so thoroughly, but it didn't stop when the bastard finally left. It hung about, prolonging whatever it was that Cian did to him. Brennan thought he had an idea that this didn't have to take so long. Cian was drawing things out because he wanted to.

What had Cian been doing? Most of the magic that had been used on him was magic that he couldn't identify. It also had a dark sense, almost like a bad smell, Brennan thought. Not that the magic actually smelled, but he could feel the darkness that was intertwined with everything Cian did.

He wondered whether that was the spells themselves, or the fact that Cian operated out of anger. Maybe a bit of both. Something to ask Taranath about, when he saw him again.

If he saw Taranath again.

As heartened as he was to know that Iris and Drake were coming for him, he wasn't sure how long he could hang on. He was barely fed, and his clothing, which had been light sleeping clothes, were in tatters. He was lucky that he had a habit of having the mirror with him at all times. Not that he'd heard from Drake or Iris again. A fact which he was both grateful for and disappointed with all at the same time.

There was a frightened little creature that he couldn't identify who came in occasionally to care for him, although he had no idea how long he'd been there. Brennan made sure he tucked the mirror under his leg when the creature was tending to him. He thought it might be a goblin of sorts, but the poor thing never looked up, and he had an overwhelming feeling of sadness and fear when he? She? It? Was near. He slept when he could, to keep up his strength, so what day it might be was beyond him at the moment.

The door cracked open. Brennan found that he

could hear much more than he'd ever been able to with restricted sight. That and he kept his eyes closed as much as possible.

It was the mystery woman. He could tell by her soft tread.

"What are you saying to him? He's fit for nothing tonight."

He tried to shrug and winced. "The truth. He's not good enough for all the people who are acting on his behalf."

"Are you trying to make him kill you slowly?"

"Better than killing me quickly," he shot back.

Her face came into view, and to his surprise, he could see a small smile on the corners of her lips. "You're making him very angry, so kudos to you."

"Is he that angry?" The thought pleased him.

"Stomping about, blasting everything in his way, and muttering a lot of hate," she replied.

Something about her speech—what was it? It tugged at his memory, but he couldn't place it. Not when he was so tired.

"You're doing well. Normally those he works on are dead by now," she continued. "I have a little bit of hope that you might make it."

"Doesn't he plan to kill me?"

"You're lucky she's not here."

He noticed that she didn't answer his question,

which answered it. Knowing that Cian meant to kill him didn't bother him as much as he thought it might. He felt confident that he might be able to hang on, but his failing strength, and the fact that Cian was harming him with who knew what shook his faith a little. Even as it made him angry, he wasn't familiar with what it was that Cian did to him.

"By she, do you mean Ailla?"

"Shhh! Big dolt! Don't say her name! Bad enough I have to be around her all the time!"

"Why?" He lowered his voice. He could hear the real fear in hers.

"I've known that one my entire life, and she is mean as can be."

He tried to turn his head to look at her, and could only move it enough to see part of her face.

"Who are you? What are you? Why have I never seen you?"

"Spend much time in the Dragon Realm?" She muttered, not meeting his eyes, poking at him and making him wince.

"No, they aren't very friendly to those of the other Realms," he said.

"Ever wonder why?"

He shook his head a little. "No. Whenever those of the Dragon Court came to my father's court, they were abrupt, and not welcoming of friendly overtures."

"Eilor with them?"

"Of course. Why wouldn't he be?"

"Well, then, with all that is going on, oh Goblin King," she looked at him, and he could see the mockery in her eyes, "Make sense why they might not be all that friendly?"

He started to speak and stopped. Of course. It made perfect sense. "Are you saying that this is not the work of the entire Dragon Court?"

She had turned her attention to his hands. "They are not as they seem. Eilor is a bastard, and there won't be much mourning when he's gone."

"He's threatened them?"

"You're quick, do you know that? Won your lady's heart easily, didn't you?"

He almost replied to her. "You're very annoying. Are you aware of that?"

To his surprise, she laughed, and it sounded genuine. "I've been told worse by far worse than you, Goblin King. If I weren't who I was, I'd have managed to get away long ago."

"When are you going to tell me who you are?"

"When you finally get away. Speaking of that, I have a request."

"I'm not exactly in the best position to grant requests, madam," he said formally.

"I'd have helped you regardless, as anyone those

two," he knew she meant Cian and Ailla, "Hate is probably good, but I want you to take me with you when you go."

"How will I get you away? How can you be sure I'll be able to get away?" He didn't want to let on that he knew Iris and Drake were coming for him.

"People love you. They will find you." She sounded very sure.

For some reason, that made him feel better.

"I know you got Carlianah out. She was scared to death, and now she's safe. I know you and your brother managed it. I'm asking for the same."

"How do you know Carlianah?" He didn't think anyone knew that she was Drake's contact and he wasn't going to out the girl. She'd risked a lot for them.

"Where do you think she gets her latest news from?"

His mouth fell open, and he turned his head as far as he could to see her. "That's you? Aine?" He whispered. He hoped on all the gods that this woman was what she presented herself as, or he'd just doomed Carlianah.

And probably everyone else he cared about.

Iris

"*I* need to walk outside, if you please," Drake said to me.

I nodded. Steam was nearly coming out of his ears. Everyone watched him stalk from the room, his shoulders stiff. I got the impression he was dying to beat the shit out of something.

"Who is the guy with the scar?" Max asked.

I shot a look towards Taranath. I wasn't sure how much I wanted to tell. He gave a little nod of his head, and that made me feel better. Even though I was supposedly the one in charge, I felt like I needed to make sure I wasn't making a mistake.

Max watched us intently. I got the impression he didn't miss much. I took a deep breath.

"I don't know for sure, but I would bet the guy with the scar is Cian, Brennan's brother." The anger that Drake felt washed over me and my hands clenched. What the hell was that ass doing here?

"I don't know who either of these people are," Max said.

"Brennan is the Goblin King—"

"Is he missing?"

I wasn't expecting that and hesitated. "Well..." How to walk this back?

Max held up a hand. "I understand not wanting to

advertise that. I'll give you my word that I won't use this information in a way that will hurt you."

"But you might use it?" Taranath asked.

Max shrugged. "My responsibility is to my pack."

"Pack? What kind of shifters are you?" I had to know. Really? I knew where my mind went, but...really?

"We are wolves."

"I thought werewolves were just a story!"

Kirk laughed. "And so are fairies," he said.

Sandy Hair joined in.

"Fae," I snapped. "Fairies have wings. Fae don't. Keep up."

That stopped both of them, which made me smirk. I know it wasn't mature, but they were like annoying brothers. Or Drake, when I first met him.

Oh, shit. I'm not doing a good job of being a good rep for the fae. I met Max's eyes, and he grinned, just a little. Maybe I wasn't the only one who found them annoying.

"Careful," Max said, glancing over his shoulder at the other two men. "If your guy out there—" he motioned towards the window, "Is any indication, fae aren't little sweet things."

I stood. "What is he doing?"

Kirk came to stand next to me.

Drake was swinging his sword, and I could tell that

he was talking, but I couldn't hear him. Probably couldn't understand him anyway, as he tended to swear in Fae. Bushes and plants flew with each swing.

"That's a wicked sword," Sandy Hair joined us. "Your mom is not going to be happy about her bushes getting whacked like that," he added towards Kirk.

"Better than the sticks you use, Dean," Kirk said.

"Bo staff," Dean corrected, not taking his eyes off Drake. "Maybe we'll have to reassess the fae...ries." He gave me a side glance that was pure evil asshat.

I rolled my eyes, finding I liked the snark from both of them. "I'd bet on Drake against you two in whatever form even if he had a broken arm and was drunk," I said.

Which made them both laugh.

"We can arrange that," Dean said. "Your Majesty."

"I don't know how your boss hasn't left you both on a highway somewhere. Or at the bottom of a well," I said, walking back to my seat. "I'm sorry, by the way," I directed this at Max. "We'll take care of the damage."

Taranath rose. "I can probably fix this easily. Once Lord Drake has returned," he peered out the window, "I'll go and see what must be done."

"With what? Your magic wand?" Dean hooted.

Taranath and I just looked at him.

"You're kidding," He started.

"You turn furry, and you're all bothered by a

wand?" I shook my head. I turned back to Max. "I'll accept your word that you will not use this information to hurt us, but why would you use the info anyway? The fae generally don't bother the Human Realm."

"Except you're here, and the brother and his woman were here six days ago," Max said. "Who knows when information will be helpful?"

I sighed. I couldn't expect an instant ally, although it sure would be nice at this point. We could use some luck, something going right.

"Fair enough," I said. "If you see Cian—the guy with the scar again, stay away from him. He's crazy, and he's very skilled magically."

"He's using very old magic in conjunction with dragon magic, which is not good for someone in his state," Taranath added.

"Dragon magic?" Max asked, one eyebrow up. "Do we need to worry about dragons, too?"

"I would have thought no, but I don't know," I said honestly. "I have no idea what Cian has planned. I know he is working to take control of all the Realms."

"How many Realms are there?" Max frowned.

"The Goblin Realm, the Dragon Realm, the Dwarf Realm, the Troll Realm, and then the Fae Realm. The Fae King is the leader of all the Realms, although each one has their own King."

Max opened his mouth, then closed it and shook his head. "I was going to ask for more about it, but it doesn't matter. They've all been around for a while, right?"

I nodded.

"And this is the first time I've seen anything, or even heard anything, so obviously you all keep to yourselves. But why is Key—key?"

"Cian?" I supplied.

"Yes, Cian," he said, saying it correctly. "Why is he here? Who's the woman with him?"

"She's pretty hot," said Dean.

"Dark hair, pale skin, and really red lips?" I asked. Dean nodded.

"Yeah, well, she's pretty like poison. That sounds like Ailla, the daughter of the Dragon King, and equally insane. She's mean as shit, and she'd off you without even thinking about it."

"She make a move on your man?" Dean asked.

"No, I booted her ass out of the way," I said.

A moment of silence, and then all of them laughed, even Taranath.

"This is a good sign, I think," Drake said, entering the room.

"You better?" I looked him up and down.

He looked flushed but less tense than he had.

"Yes, ladyship, I am. Your bushes, however, have

suffered. We shall take responsibility for them," Drake looked at Max.

"I am off to see to it now," Taranath rose. "Sit, Lord Drake." He glided from the room.

How did he look so graceful? It was like he had wheels under his robes.

"What'd I miss?" Drake fell into the chair.

"I was trying to warn them about Cian and Ailla," I said.

"He's probably insane," Drake frowned. "I'm not sure that Ailla is truly sane, either."

"She can fake nice really well," I added. "So just leave them be. Please. It's better that they think they're moving around this Realm without notice."

"So why did you end up here, if you didn't know the other guy had been here?" Kirk asked.

I liked that Max, who was clearly the boss, let the other two talk. It said a lot about him as the leader.

"I told you, it was an accident. I'm not great at portal travel, and—"

"Sometimes misdirection happens when people are learning," Drake finished.

That was nice and totally unexpected. I shot him a grateful smile.

"You let a newb drive when you're in a hurry?" Dean asked.

"Is there a better way to learn?" Drake didn't take offense.

Apparently, beating the hell out of bushes had made him a new person, or something. I needed to remember when he got his knickers in a twist that I could suggest something similar.

I wondered if this was something that Brennan needed, too. Thoughts of him were dangerous. I kept myself focused and under control by not dwelling on him—my Brennan—too much. The idea of Brennan going outside and beating up bushes made me smile, which totally didn't fit the situation at hand. I missed him so much.

"Nope," Max said. He and Drake smiled, just a little.

Maybe we'd get out of here without testosterone killing anyone.

"Hey!" Dean darted to the window again. "What is your guy doing?"

Drake didn't move, and I made myself keep still.

"Fixing the damage," Drake said.

"Wow," Dean said.

"Are you witches?" Max asked.

"No. We're fae. Fae do magic. It's not only witches who use it," Drake answered.

I was content to let him take this. I had no idea and didn't want to say the wrong thing.

"Why don't we know about you?"

"Because we don't want you to. As well, humans don't fare well in the Fae Realm."

"What does that mean?" Max leaned forward, interested.

"It means most humans die," I said.

"But you're not dying. We'd be able to tell if you were," Kirk frowned.

"I'm part fae," I began.

"How does that happen?" Dean asked.

"Um, my grandmother is fae?" I debated being shitty and decided against it.

"There's obviously a lot more at play here than we realized," Max said, and I saw the leader in him take over.

"Listen," I held up a hand to forestall more questions. "You're right. But Drake wasn't kidding. We really are on a schedule here. We have to go. Will you make a bargain with me?" I improvised. I could tell that Max wasn't keen on letting us leave just yet, as nice as he'd been. He reminded me a lot of Drake. Although with somewhat better manners.

"Maybe."

"I will communicate with you once we find who we're looking for. I promise. Brennan and I both will. And we'll answer all your questions." I ignored Drake's noise of protest next to me. "In return, I ask that you keep away from Cian and Ailla if you see either of them again. And let me know."

"This Realm is not here, right?"

"Right."

"How will I communicate?"

I turned to Drake. "I know you have one."

"No, Iris!" I could tell he was angry because he used my name.

"This is important, Drake! Cian being here is something we never even considered! Why is he here? It makes me nervous, and if we have someone here who can let us know when he shows up—with Ailla, no less! You can bet your ass her dad knows!"

"That's no worse than Cian knowing!" He protested.

"I think it's way worse! Eilor knows Cian is batshit, and he's gone along with it all this time! And what he and Ailla did to Brennan, and you? Are you kidding? He's like the evil mastermind behind this, using crazy Cian as the cover!"

Max, Kirk, and Dean watched us like we were a tennis match, their heads moving back and forth as Drake and I argued. Taranath came in and stood at the door, hands clasped in front of him. He reminded me of a smiling Spock.

He might be my ally in this, too. I turned to him.

"Tell him, Taranath! It makes sense to have an ally here!"

Dean said, "Hey, no one said we're allies!"

"Dean," Max glared at him.

Dean left the room.

Drake also looked at Taranath, clearly expecting support. "The mirrors are for the royal family. We don't hand them out like party favors!"

"Like you even know what a party favor is!" I shot back, frustrated.

"Oh, really, ladyship? I doubt you even know what a party is!" Drake leaned in. He was just as angry as I was.

If I hadn't been so mad at his pigheadedness, I could appreciate how alike we are. And how we both loved Brennan so very much. I was sure Drake felt as shitty as I did.

This was about Brennan. "Drake, we need all the help we can get," I said, all anger gone.

"Her Majesty is not wrong, my lord," Taranath said. "The ability to communicate with this Realm will be helpful, now that we know Cian has been here."

Drake didn't say anything, and I knew he was struggling with the idea that I was right. I hated to be wrong, so I understood and kept quiet.

"Fine!" He stood up and wrenched the mirror from

the pouch at his side. "But you will get me another, your Majesty!"

I took it from him, standing as I did, and placed my hand on his. "Drake, we'll find him." I knew exactly how he felt. I patted his hand a couple of times, feeling like my mom, finally understanding why she did it. Maybe it would make him feel a little better, as it had when my mom did it to me.

Then I handed it to Max. "When you want to speak to me, say my name, and just wait. If anyone other than me shows up in the mirror, turn it over immediately."

He looked at the mirror. At that moment, Dean came in, eating a piece of pie.

"That's what all the fuss was about? A mirror? Really?"

"Depth is totally lost on you, isn't it?" I asked.

"What?" He said with his mouth full.

Kirk cuffed him in the side of the head. "Go back to the kitchen, man. You're hopeless."

"You want a piece?"

This time Max gave him the stink eye, and he disappeared again. When Dean was gone, Max looked at me. "This is a big deal, isn't it?"

I nodded. "Drake isn't exaggerating. Only the royal family and a few others use them. But this is for the royal family, so I think it's a worthwhile cause."

"You're pretty trusting of people you don't know."

"I think I know you well enough," I said, giving him the eyeball. "And I think you understand what it means to give your word. I have yours that you will not use your knowledge of us in any manner that will cause us harm, and I will not ask you to put your pack in danger. But you will let me know if he shows up, and Brennan and I will return when this is all done." I stuck out my hand. I had a feeling about him. That he was worth the trust. In spite of his reticence. I got the impression he felt the same. Well, we'll see, won't we?

He looked down at my hand, which, I had to admit, with the horse riding, and then the cave mishap in the Troll Realm, was looking sketchy at best. Certainly, not anything like a queen ought to look. Then he looked up at me and took my hand, shaking it firmly.

"We'll let you know if we see or sense him again. Now that we have the scent of him, and of you, we know what to pay attention for."

"Will you keep the knowledge of us to yourself?"

Kirk made a motion that indicated he didn't like the question, and Max made a noise in his throat—a growl—that startled me. Kirk looked down.

"Normally, I might hesitate to agree to such a request. As the leader of the pack in this territory, I communicate with other pack leaders. But for the time, I will keep your existence to myself. After I talk with you and Brennan, I may not be able to keep quiet."

Now it was Drake's turn to sound agitated.

"Fair enough," I said. "We need to leave. I've delayed us long enough."

"Very true," Drake muttered.

"Is there enough room to portal from here?" I asked. "I don't want to be outside in the open where we might be seen. Who knows if Cian has someone lurking around here?"

Drake smiled ruefully. "I hate to admit it, ladyship, but that is sound reasoning. I think we can portal safely from here. I also think you should let one of us do it," He added.

"Yes, please! I'm tired of landing us in all the wrong places!"

"And here I thought we were newfound allies, all set to hold hands and sing Kumbaya," Max said. "I'm disappointed, crushed even."

I glanced at him and realized that he was kidding. It was hard to tell since he seemed to sport a serious face all the time.

"You're not going to break shit up, are you?" Kirk asked.

Drake rolled his eyes. "Really, why do you assume we're uncivilized? Just step back, please."

Max and Kirk moved back towards the door.

"All right, ladyship, pay attention. See if you can figure out what you've been doing wrong," Drake said as he pulled a stone from his pouch. "I am focusing on the castle that we saw on the map." He looked down at his hand, and I could see a glow even though the stone was covered by his fingers.

Taranath stood closer to us, and I tucked an arm through his. He seemed startled at my familiarity, but at this point, he was family to me. I could feel the ripples moving around me, although nothing worse.

I glanced over at Max and Kirk as Dean poked his head in the door. "Thank you," I said.

And then we were in a forest in the dark.

12

Brennan

"Who are you?" He whispered. He and Drake had talked about her, this spy, this Aine, and the thought that Eilor was breeding dragons with the fae, or humans, or at all horrified him. They'd been captured and kept under tight control for a reason. Dragons had nearly ended all of the Realms.

"I am myself. What do you mean?" Her voice was careful and very neutral.

"Drake told me a bit about you. Who are your parents?"

Her hesitation told him that Drake had gotten

some of it, at least, correct. Otherwise, she'd name her parents like any other fae.

"I don't know my mother. She died when I was born. I've never met my father, either. But I'm told he was part dragon. My mother, I don't know much about." Her voice dropped. "I think she may have been human."

"Not fae, then?"

He could see her shake her head out of the side of his view. Small flashes of the green light from the spell she'd used before flared as she healed him. He felt better, revived somewhat. Brennan paid attention to the magic she used. It had that unknown sense that Cian's did, so she must have learned similar spells. But hers lacked the dark shadow he felt when Cian employed it against him.

"I don't know. Even though she died when I was born, I'm told, I can remember a woman with long hair leaning over me. Nanny tells me it was her, but...I don't know."

While she kept her tone even, Brennan could tell that the lack of knowledge bothered her. He understood. Not knowing landed high on his list of irritations.

"Can you tell me what you do know?"

"Why do you ask?"

Now he heard wariness in her words. Perhaps she

regretted being so open with a veritable stranger. "Because I am interested. I was interested when I heard of you before. Your existence has been kept very secret, mistress."

She snorted. "I am not surprised. Eilor doesn't want anyone to know what he and Princess are up to."

"What are they up to?"

"They—" she stopped as they both heard the sounds in the hall.

The green light winked out, and he heard her swear softly. He closed his eyes, frustrated that he couldn't help her, and knowing that he needed to appear as pathetic as he did when Cian left him earlier. Which made him even more frustrated than his too-short conversation with his mystery benefactor. He concentrated on letting his muscles go slack and allowing how tired he felt, in spite of the healing, come to the forefront.

Brennan could feel the mirror dig into his leg, and it gave him strength. This girl, Aine, was right. They would come for him because they loved him. He hoped she was able to hide.

"Well, isn't this a lovely sight," Ailla's voice grated on his ears. "Time to wake up, your Majesty."

Iris

"*W*ell?" I whispered. "Are we here?"

"Of course we are," Drake took a few steps away from where we'd landed.

I noticed that the more we traveled via portal, the less it looked like an opening. It just sort of... happened. I wondered if Brennan had made it look that way with me early on because it was easier. Something I'd need to ask about. This seemed more like we just drifted to a new place. Interesting.

"We have arrived, your Majesty," Taranath said.

"Okay," I whispered, not wanting to speak any louder. The place felt oppressive. "What now?"

"We need to assess the castle's defenses, and then proceed from there." Drake sounded all business.

"That's it? Your grand plan is to storm the castle?"

"You have a better idea?" Now he sounded pissed.

"Not at the moment, but really, Drake? Storm the castle?"

"I am open and ready to hear your suggestions," he dropped his pack on the ground and began to dig around in it.

I was pleased to see that my bag had made it as well, and I took the few steps towards him and picked it up, feeling oddly reassured by just holding it.

The Fae Realm was making me weirder and weirder. I felt overwhelmed with strong feelings, what my dad would call gut instinct. It was all over the place. I'd been listening to it since we'd left the Goblin Castle, and it hadn't steered me wrong yet. Maybe this was part of the becoming more fae?

As Drake went through his things looking for who knows what, I sat down next to Taranath, who'd found a rock. Still holding my bag, I made myself as comfortable as I could.

"Can I ask you something while we're waiting for the plan?"

"Of course."

"I'm noticing my, well, what I'd call gut instinct getting stronger and louder. Like with Dhysara, I knew it would be best for me to talk to her, or that I just know it was a good idea to leave the mirror with Max. Is that part of being here?"

Taranath turned to look at me. "I can't say for sure, my lady. I am going to give it my best guess and say, probably. You're an anomaly as far as my knowledge goes. I can't be sure of anything for you going forward. But if you've never noticed something before, this or anything else, yes. It's probably a result of being in Fae longer."

"Do you think I'm going to die?" This still bothered me, outside of Brennan's dreams of the Eidolan.

"No, I do not."

"You sound pretty sure."

His face dropped. "I have tended children wished to the Goblin King, my lady. I know the signs of a human who is failing."

"Oh. I'm sorry," I offered.

Taranath smiled a somber smile that made him look old.

"How old are you?" I asked.

"I am five hundred and twenty-seven."

"You've seen a lot of children, haven't you?"

He nodded slowly. "Not as many as you might think, although I will confess, more than I care for. Sometimes, the children do survive, and when they do, they are adopted by the fae."

"Which is a good thing, right?"

"Yes."

"So why is there a lot of crap about Drake being the Fae King?"

Taranath sighed. "That's different, Iris. There would be an outcry if Brennan were chosen to succeed his father, with you as his wife. The nobles of the Realms won't care as they see him as only the Goblin King. And Brennen will never be anything else."

"Doesn't someone have to be chosen for it?"

He nodded again. "There is no one who has shown the aptitude, and Drake isn't interested, even if he had it. Although most feel Drake is the unofficial heir, and everyone involved is content for that belief to stand. It will be interesting," he looked away, tapping his chin, "To see what happens when there is a royal birth. I know so little of what is to come for you that this may be the time when a child will succeed their father to this particular throne." He lapsed into silence.

I let him sit and then said, "Okay but where does that leave me, at this moment? You think following my gut is a good idea?"

"It hasn't led you wrong yet, has it?"

"No."

He leaned over and patted my hand. "Then keep going with it until it does. That is the best advice I can give." He stood. "My lord, have you devised our next moves? May I be of help?"

What? What the hell? I remembered that when I most wanted to strangle Taranath was in the middle of some lesson. He was the easily the most irritating teacher I'd ever had. But he'd given me the reassurance that I wanted, that I needed. I could trust this.

What I hadn't said, and honestly, what I was afraid to say, was that I might be under some spell that made me choose the wrong thing, make bad decisions. It sounded stupid even when I thought it, but I remembered how crazy I felt while under Ailla's spell. Nothing made sense, everything made me pissed off, and I didn't trust anyone close to me at all. I didn't want to end up there again.

It was a possibility since we were walking into the lion's den. But Brennan was there, and that made it worth the risk. I knew that he'd move all the Realms to get to me. Could I do any less?

Well, to hell with Ailla. I wasn't going to let her scare me, or make me afraid. I mean, I had a healthy dose of fear. I'm not stupid. But I wasn't going to let the fear rule me. One of the good things about having to do this with Drake and Taranath was that it left me little time to sit and doubt or worry. There just was no time for it.

I got up and went to where they had their heads together.

"What can I do to help?"

They both turned to look at me, Drake speaking as he did so.

"Stay behind us, and try not to get hurt. Brennan will kill me if you do."

I glared.

"I think you need to focus on doing protection overall," Taranath said. "I will be working with Lord Drake to get to the king, so it will be hard for me to shield us both. You're good with that particular spell, and I trust your judgment." He smiled.

I returned it, thinking on what we'd just talked about.

None of this went over well with Drake, of course. God, he was such a wet blanket.

"You think she is up to this, Taranath? It's our lives you're betting on it."

"You know I can do this," I said. "Start treating me like something other than an unwanted accessory."

He frowned, even as Taranath spoke.

"I think she is extremely capable with this spell. More of the fighting spells, no, she's not up to par with you and I. Iris has several that she can use should she need them, and you are an advocate of learning as you go, correct?"

The expression on Drake's face was priceless. Maybe he shouldn't spout his opinion so much. I tried not to snicker.

"Please stay behind us, Iris. I want to keep you safe."

Such a statement was restrained from Drake. And he was sincere.

"I won't put myself in danger," I began, and stopped when I saw the frown come back. "Well, not more than I am already in, how about that? I promise."

"I'll hold you to that," he muttered. "Get yourself ready. Do you want a stone? That helps with focus in fights."

"Um, yeah." I wasn't used to him treating me as an equal, and all of a sudden, this got real. Real real. I

knew that Ailla would kill me. I didn't know about
Cian, but that was because he'd want to hold capturing
me over Brennan's head. I felt my stomach lurch, and
my palms began to sweat.

"It will be fine, your Majesty," Taranath murmured.

I couldn't speak. The worry, the self-doubt, the
reality of this was all hitting like a ton of bricks. This
must be what a ton of bricks felt like. He patted my
shoulder, and then let me be.

It was what I needed. Drake reached across to me
and handed me two stones. "Just in case," he said, his
typical mocking grin back in place.

That's one thing you could say for Drake. He didn't
hold grudges—well, not for too long. I took them,
wrapping my hand around them, feeling the warmth
of them. Which was odd. I looked down at them—they
didn't look any different, but they were warm. I slid one
into a pocket and kept the other one in hand.

I had to take a deep breath. I could feel my heart start
to race a little, and I was holding the stone so tightly that
my fingernails were digging into my palm. I stretched out
my neck, and then my arms, breathing deeply as I did so.

I could do this.

"All right, we're going to go in through the
northwest door on the outside of the castle, the one
that—" Drake began.

"The back door," I said. "Got it. How far to where we think Brennan is?"

Drake shook his head. "I'm not sure. I haven't been here, so it's the best guess. I would suppose that they don't want the Goblin King hanging about the dinner table, so he's going to be somewhere private, a small room that is hidden away somewhere. We're going to have to sneak in."

"All this magic and we're sneaking in," I shook my head. "If you've never been here before, where are we going to sneak into? How do you know where the back door is?"

"We follow the smell."

"What?" This idea didn't make sense.

"The smell. The back door, as you put it, is where all the garbage and waste from the castle is sent."

"The...waste?" I was getting a bad feeling about this.

"Yes, Iris. The waste. From the kitchen, the garden--"

"The bathroom?" I interrupted.

"That too," Drake grinned.

Why did he have to look evilly gleeful? Jerk.

"Oh, lovely. Well, since you're such an expert, lead the way," I gestured towards the castle.

"What? You don't wish to exercise the privilege of

ladies first?" He turned, and I could hear him laughing as he finished his sentence.

"Not in this case. I am more than happy to stay behind."

"Perhaps we could maintain silence as we get closer to what is no doubt an enemy castle?" Taranath asked. The question was mild, but it hit home.

Drake and I shut up.

How had I gotten to the point where we were sneaking in through the sewers?

13

Brennan

*H*e looked at Ailla. She didn't look as polished as she normally did. Her eyes were bright, and her smile seemed too wide somehow. It made her look a little crazed. Perhaps spending so much uninterrupted time with Cian did that.

Or maybe she was, in fact, crazed. Maybe she'd merely hidden it from him the few times he saw her before and after their betrothal. Whatever the truth was, he felt he saw the true Ailla before him, and she was rather scary.

He remembered something his father had told him long ago—that people who were crazed felt they had nothing to lose. But Ailla, in conjunction with Cian, had much to lose. And much to gain. Much hinged on her doing whatever her plans with Cian demanded she do.

"I am awake," he said, keeping his voice level. "What can I do for you, Ailla?"

"That's 'Your Highness' to you, Brennan," she sneered. "You're not the king anymore."

He raised his eyebrows. "Really? I was unaware that changing my location removed me from the throne. What a fascinating idea, Ailla." He couldn't help the sarcasm that crept out.

"We've taken the throne from you. Even now," She grinned and he saw the madness come out completely on her face, "Those loyal to Cian and I are entering the Goblin Realm. They will be assuming the throne. And why not? The king has abandoned his realm in the time of need!"

"They will never believe such a thing. It appears we have different ideas of loyalty, Ailla."

"Really?" One corner of her mouth lifted.

Brennan hated the smug look she gave him. "Really."

"Then why is it that your loyal," she put great emphasis on the word, "Subjects recently tried to kill you, and that human fool you dare to call brother?"

Brennan allowed himself to feel pride at the way he managed his temper as an adult. Ever since the accident with Cian, he'd put great effort into not being angry, not letting anger overshadow his emotions. It was a bit easier when he knew she was trying to goad him, looking for a response.

"There are people who will make mistakes when they are laboring under a misapprehension," Brennan said, keeping his voice level and calm. "I don't judge my entire kingdom by a few misguided subjects."

Ailla laughed. "You can think that if it makes you feel better," she said. "But it won't change the facts, Brennan!"

Brennan forced himself to look around the room as though he were bored. It was difficult because Ailla kept moving all over the place. It seemed as though she couldn't keep herself still. When he made eye contact with her, Brennan was shocked to see the insanity in her eyes.

As she paced, Ailla wrung her hands in front of her, glancing at him quickly. Her head moved back and forth like a bird. Brennan couldn't tell if she was looking for the right words to taunt him with, or if she was so caught up, she couldn't speak.

Her gown was a bright contrast to the dark stone walls. A feeble sun shone through the small window. Brennan wished again for the thousandth time that the sunlight would reach where he was tied to the table.

Ailla finally opened her mouth, fixing her eyes on

Brennan. They shone with the fire of her feelings. "You thought you had it all together, didn't you? You thought marrying me would tie it all up for you. You'd have the Dragon Realm under your thumb, my father and I under your thumb, and life would just be perfect for the Goblin King!"

Brennan could feel the tingling across his skin. It was as though small lightning bolts decided to dance on him. As he looked at Ailla, he realized she was the source of the lightning bolt tingling. She continued, speaking to him with great triumph, but he no longer heard her words.

He had not seen Aine since Ailla had come in. As he had not seen the whole of the room, he didn't know where she could have hidden. He was afraid that Ailla might be able to see his thoughts or read his mind, so he deliberately shoved the thoughts of his visitor away.

But where had she gone? He'd heard nothing from where she'd stood next to him since the door opened. Ailla had said nothing either, and she would not have let that pass unnoticed. She would not have kept quiet about finding Aine within. He felt sure that Ailla would have done her worst against his benefactor. He was glad she had seemingly escaped, but he wanted to know that she was safe.

His attention returned to Ailla, who was still speaking. He allowed himself to focus on her, without hearing anything that she said. He'd already learned that regardless of what Ailla wanted, Cian wouldn't let anything happen not of his making. He watched Ailla as she continued to pace, her words become more ranting and rambling with each passing moment. Even with the insanity she spouted, she still *looked* beautiful.

Although he had to note, less and less so every time he saw her.

His thoughts diverted from his concerns when he thought about Drake. He was very glad that Drake was not here to see Ailla. In spite of all of his of statements to the contrary, Brennan knew you didn't just turn off love. Not even one the one you loved was as insane as could be.

"I hope you've been listening, Brennan," Ailla sneered with a strong emphasis on his name. "If you think this is bad, you have no understanding of what real suffering is."

Brennan said nothing, only raised an eyebrow. He knew that Ailla hated to be dismissed. He'd done this to her before while they were still engaged. When he thought she was normal, and his less-than-ardent attention had been an accident. She had reacted poorly, in a way that seemed very extreme for such a mild infraction.

He felt the tingling rise along his arms and neck once more. It didn't take much to make her angry. The tingling sensation let him know that he hit his mark and infuriated her.

A genuine smile broke out across his face. It pleased him to no end to know that Ailla wanted to hurt him badly. But her fear of Cian kept her from it. Knowing that he taunted her, and she was powerless to indulge her desires. He almost laughed at the anger and frustration she made no effort to conceal.

"Keep laughing, your Majesty," she hissed. "It won't be long before you are never able to smile again."

Her words sent a chill across him that could not be dispelled by the sunny day or the warmth of the room. Nevertheless, he kept a smile on his face. He wouldn't let her see the effect of her words.

If he got angry, she won. She would use it as an excuse to hurt him. And he felt a stubborn sense of satisfaction at denying her the thing she wanted. If he was going to die, which he had no intention of doing, it wasn't going to be at the hands of a crazed woman.

Ailla made a noise that sounded very much between a huff and a shriek. Muttering to herself, she stormed from the room. The door slammed behind her, a testament to how angry she was.

The silence that he been enjoying before her appearance fell across the room again, and Brennan closed his eyes, hoping for a little warmth of the sun to reach the rest of the room.

"Well, you certainly have a death wish." Aine's voice said in his ear.

"Does it matter what kind of wish that I have? Cian and Ailla have already decided what is going to happen to me," said Brennan, trying not to grin. He couldn't believe how pleased he was that not only was Aine safe; she hadn't left him. "Where did you hide?"

"I ducked under your table here, and then used a cloaking spell," Aine replied. "She was so mad at you; she didn't pay any attention to anything else in the room."

Spite of the seriousness of his situation, and the very real fear that he might not make it, Brennan found himself holding in a laugh. "She was pretty angry, wasn't she? It was all I could do not to make it worse."

"I think you did a good job making things worse without even trying," said Aine with a dry tone in her voice. "I'd hate to see what happened if you really sought to make her angry."

"Thank you for staying," Brennan said quietly, all laughter gone. "It makes it easier to withstand her when I don't feel so alone." He felt very vulnerable making such a confession. Before meeting Iris, he would've never said such a thing to anyone, not even Drake. But now, after being strapped to this table for who knows how long he felt pride was a virtue he could not afford to have. Aine had helped him so much already; there was no sense in hiding from her.

"You're going to take me with you," she said. "You promised, remember? When they come for you, you can't leave me here."

Brennan could hear the desperation in her voice. The mocking, calm manner she frequently had disappeared when she talked about leaving with him. He felt a concern he hadn't felt before. Did she expect something more from him? He hoped he had not inadvertently given himself a romantic entanglement. He chose his next words carefully.

"Iris and I will be happy to give you a home in the Goblin Realm," Brennan spoke slowly. "I know that she will be forever grateful for all that you've done for me. As am I," he finished.

Aine gave out an incredibly unladylike snort. "Whatever are you thinking, Goblin King?" Brennan could hear the laughter in her tone. "That's all I want from you," she added. "I need a place to hide away, to make sure that Cian and Ailla never find me again. I don't want Eilor to find me again either," she added.

"Eilor? What does he have to do any of this?" Concern over appearances vanished immediately at the mention of Eilor.

He felt, rather than saw, Aine stand and come closer to him. Unlike most other times he saw her, she stood in his line of vision. The expression on her face was grave and worried. She made sure to make eye contact and then spoke.

"What does Eilor have to do with this? Are you honestly that uninformed?"

Brennan opened his mouth to speak when he froze. He could feel the tingling throughout his body again, although not the sort that signaled the danger that Ailla or sometimes Cian brought.

"Iris?" he said out loud. He didn't mean to say her name. He didn't want her name associated with anything about this place. He didn't want her name anywhere near the likes of Cian or Ailla. But the sensation was so intense that he spoke before he even thought.

"What you talking about?" asked Aine. The tone of her voice suggested he was mad.

Iris

I put my hand over my mouth for what seemed like the hundredth time. The smell in here really could not get any worse. I didn't even know such a horrible smell existed, but here it was. We were right in the middle of I had to keep my head down anyway, so that I didn't step in anything completely gross and throw up all over the place.

"Great idea," I muttered. "This was so fabulous."

Drake didn't even turn around, but he'd heard me. "Sorry your ladyship," he shot back. "All the other entrances were unavailable."

As if to punish me for my ill humor, my foot slipped, and I had to put a hand out and touch the wall. Slimy doesn't even begin to describe it. I snatched my hand back but stopped short of wiping my hand on my clothing. My hand hovered, as though belonging to someone else, in front of me.

"Taranath, do you have something I can use to wipe my hands?" I waggled my hand at him even though I knew he couldn't see me in the dim light.

Again, without turning around, Taranath passed a piece of cloth over his shoulder. He couldn't look back. We all had to watch where we stepped. I wondered if the smell would sink into my skin. It was that strong.

"When do you think the last time was that they cleaned this?" I asked.

"Probably never," Drake said from in front of Taranath. "This is not a castle that is used all year round, and the staff just isn't here to keep things clean. Plus, it's Eilor's castle. I'm starting to wonder if he does anything in a reasonable fashion."

"What?" I stopped, and looked around to see — to

see what? There was nothing to see, other than slime and filth and horrible smell that made my nose want to fall off my face.

But — something else was there. "Brennan?" I asked wonderingly.

That made both Drake and Taranath stop in their tracks. They turned around carefully so as not to fall into the gross nastiness.

"Did you see Brennan?" Drake asked me.

I nodded, although I knew he couldn't see me in this light. "For a minute there, it was like — I don't know, like he was right there."

"Is that possible?" Drake asked.

"It could be him," Taranath responded slowly. "There is a lot of magic at work here. I can feel it, rather like... an underground river or stream. It's there; I just can't see it."

The tone of his voice told me that he was looking around, probably with a look of surprise on his face. I knew that look well. I'd seen it plenty of times in his rooms at the Goblin Castle.

"Can you see? Can you feel him?" Impatience laced Drake's words.

"No, I can't. I just... I just know he's here." I wished I could be sure, but there was no way to describe it. It was just a feeling, knowing that Brennan was here and close enough that we could sense one another. I

focused hard the feeling trying to pinpoint it or find
some further detail from it.

"He's... He's not in pain," I said squinting even
though I saw nothing. "He's having a lot of emotion, or
feelings?"

Drake snorted. "And thus ends another good man,"
he said dramatically. "Let them get married and it's all
downhill from there."

He's close enough to me that I'm able to reach him
when I take a swat at him. "Thanks a lot, jerk," I hissed.
"See if I try to help you again!"

Amazingly in the middle of that dark, stinky,
tunnel, we all started to laugh. It was the first time we
laughed in — I couldn't remember how long. A
while.

Taranath leaned closer to me and patted me on the
arm. "We're going to find him, Iris. I have an excellent
feeling about this."

"No one bets against Taranath!" Drake said,
striding ahead of us all. "Anyone who does usually
loses," he finished with a laugh.

We started moving forward again, and I noted that
the tunnel seemed to be angling slightly uphill. It
meant that I had to step even more carefully, so as not
to slip in the piles of disgusting whatever under my
feet. I was still thinking about what I had felt when I
sensed Brennan when Taranath stopped in front of me.

I only noticed that he stopped because I ran right into the back of him.

"Hey!"

It was Drake who answered. "Shhh," he whispered. "Look up there," he pointed.

I had to peer between him and Taranath to see what he was talking about. A thin line of light shone ahead, horizontally and below eye level. Keeping our eyes on the light, we reached the door.

"Well, what are we waiting for?" I started to push between the two of them, not bothering to keep my voice down. "Let's go! Let's not waste any more time!"

Drake stopped me as I attempted to pass by him. "No, wait, Iris! We don't want to just burst through the door—remember the Troll Realm?"

That stopped me. "You had to bring that up, didn't you?" I grumbled. But I stopped my forward movement. "So what do you suggest, oh mighty one?"

"Let's take a minute. I'll open the door, and scout the corridor, or wherever this leads to."

I heard the swish of his sword coming out of its scabbard. That slow, deliberate sound sent a chill through me that started at my feet and quickly traveled to my head. It scared me. A lot. Because this made things real.

We wouldn't be able to go back from here.

Drake moved closer to the door, and I could see

him go into a crouch, a fighter's stance. The thrill of fear that I'd felt dissipated a little. Drake knew his business.

"Taranath, can you open this? Quietly?" Drake whispered as we all stood about a foot from the door.

Taranath moved closer, and I saw a cool blue light flare up, illuminating him briefly. The fear eased even more as I watched him work calmly. He was a steady force in our group.

The lock on the door clicked. It echoed through the tunnel with the sound of an oncoming freight train— or so it seemed.

I let out a breath I didn't realize I'd been holding.

"All right, stand back," Drake said. "Let me see what's on the other side."

"Trolls," I muttered.

He shot me a look over his shoulder. "We probably would have smelled them by now."

He had a point.

Taranath stood shoulder to shoulder with me as Drake carefully pried the door open. After opening it enough to squeeze through, he stood back and waited.

It felt as though the entire castle did, too.

After an eternity of a minute, he slid along the wall—eww. That was going to leave a really stinky mark. He crouched again and slipped through the opening.

I waited for the screams, or sounds of fighting, or something.

None came.

His head reappeared in the doorway. "There's no one here. We're lucky. Have your stones ready," He said to me.

I pulled one from my pocket with fumbling fingers when he said, "Wait."

"What?" I couldn't get my voice to rise above a whisper. Until that moment, I didn't realize how truly frightened I was.

"Where's your mirror?"

"In my pocket."

"Let me have it since you gave mine away." He held out his hand, not expecting any resistance.

I didn't offer any, even though I really, really didn't want to give up my mirror. It was the one link I had to Brennan—who we're going to see shortly I reminded myself.

I couldn't think of anything beyond that.

I handed it to him, and he disappeared through the door.

"Iris, you go next. I want to be able to protect you if need be," Taranath said.

"But—"

"No buts," he interrupted. "You are the Queen, in spite of how informal we've become on this journey. I am sworn to protect you. Not to mention what the King would say."

There was enough light that I could see the faint smile on his face.

"We will get him back, Iris," He patted my hand. "Now—"

"Are we having a party before we make any move?" Drake's head and voice poked through the door. "Or do you need some special invitation to follow me while we have no obstacles?"

"Keep your hair on," I grumbled. I followed the head, which now wore an annoyed expression.

"It's a bloody gift that no one has spotted us, what with our rather lackadaisical approach to sneaking into the enemy stronghold," Drake said. "Would you please hurry up, ladyship?"

I quickened my steps to fall in behind him. It wasn't easy. He was taller and when in high emotion, as he was now, took long strides. I had to almost run to keep up. God, he could be such a jerk sometimes.

Who would die for me, or Brennan.

The thought struck me, and I slowed my pace, lurching forward when Taranath got close behind me. The walls seemed like they closed in—the warm brown of the stone no longer felt welcoming, but menacing. Our feet rang out as we hurried forward.

All this time, I'd figured we'd get Brennan, and get

back and that would be it. Even with my mishaps in portal travel, we'd had very few problems. Other than knowing whether Brennan was alive.

But now, faced with the threat of what could happen, the idea that not all of us might make it home hit me very hard.

Oh God, oh God, let it be all right. Please, please, please. Let him be safe. Please let us all get away from here safely.

We continued, moving deeper into the castle. After seeing the daily routines in the Goblin Castle, these corridors seemed deserted, eerily so. There was no life here, no décor, no staff, no anything. It was a shell. Not like my castle—and my eyes misted at the thought.

"How do you know where we're going?" I whispered to Drake's back.

"We need to find out where everyone is. They're not going to fool with having staff all throughout the castle. Not if they're trying to hide him."

Made sense. At this point, I was happy to stay in back and let someone else do the leading.

Did that make me a coward? After all, it was my husband we were seeking.

A bang of some kind around the corner from where we were stopped all of us, like a game of statues.

14

Brennan

ootsteps sounded in the corridor beyond the door. They were angry, hard, striking on the stone floor like an ax.

"Someone's coming back!" Brennan hissed at Aine. "Hide!"

Her head ducked out of his sight line just as the door slammed open, making everything in the room shudder. Brennan pretended to be sleeping, and slowly opened his eyes. He hoped with all the hope he had that Aine had managed to hide herself.

Ailla had returned.

"So, Brennan, you've been keeping secrets," she said, walking towards him with her arms crossed.

Brennan got a look at her face. She was furious. He could almost see flames of anger shooting off her. Where was Cian? It wasn't like him to allow Ailla to have this much unrestricted access to himself. Cian liked to be the one inflicting any pain or suffering that was being given out.

"I have no idea what you refer to. I am sure, however, that you'll tell me," he drawled in his most lazy manner. Better to have her angry and not entirely focused.

Even though he'd felt what he thought was Iris briefly, he couldn't wait for her and Drake to arrive. He knew better than anyone that what Cian was doing was harming him. Aine's help kept the damage at a minimum, at least physically. But Cian was draining him of...he couldn't tell what it was, exactly.

In addition to being frustrated at the fact that Cian was accomplishing something, he was angry that with all his magic, with Taranath, and all that came with being the Goblin King, he didn't know what Cian was doing. Not precisely. Not even halfway to precise, if he was honest.

So Ailla being in this room twice in one day, without Cian overseeing, put all his nerves on edge. He didn't want to admit it, but his crazed brother was proving more effective than he'd originally thought.

There was something to the idea that madness inspired and pushed.

"I hear that congratulations are in order," Ailla came close to him with a smile on her face.

That was worse than when she was angry.

She ran her fingers along his captive arm, drumming her fingers a little as though he wasn't tied up against his will. As if this was a flirtation, a trifle of interaction.

"I might need to put on a face of mourning that you've so completely gotten over me. So quickly, too, Brennan. One might call that...faithless."

Her words angered him as nothing else she'd said before did.

"Really, Ailla? I would think that you would find no room to lecture me about faithlessness," he shot back.

Whatever she'd been expecting, that wasn't it.

"What do you mean?" The question seemed to come out involuntarily.

"Pretending to love Drake. As though he wouldn't tell me," he let his eyes roll past her head and hoped that his expression looked scornful.

Something was afoot here, and he felt that if he could get Ailla off balance, he and Aine would have a chance to escape. In spite of her calm demeanor, Ailla was upset. He could feel it coming from her. But she was skilled at masking her emotion and thoughts—so he needed to get her to the point where she lost that control.

"He didn't tell you!" She burst into laughter, and Brennan could hear the tinge of anger and insanity in it. "Poor stupid human oaf, he nearly twisted himself into knots over the fact that he was so nice, too nice, to the betrothed of his beloved brother!" She laughed again.

"Well, I would presume that it felt stupid to someone who knows nothing of loyalty."

Her face was twisted. Excellent. He'd hit a nerve with her.

"You think I owed you loyalty? That I owed you anything? You didn't care about me! And I didn't wish for your affection! Why would I want that? I have the love of a powerful man—the real king, the king of all the Realms!" Her eyes looked wildly around, daring him to argue.

"Do you?" He wondered if she knew about Dhysara.

"Do I what?"

"Have the love of Cian? He doesn't seem interested in anyone other than himself. Everyone I've seen around him is only there for..." he stopped, and smiled. "Well, since you are with him far more than I, I'm sure you know." He let his head relax, and roll to the side, closing his eyes.

The slap stunned him. He found his head whipped to the other side, and looked into the eyes of a genuinely infuriated Ailla.

"What do you know of love? Of loyalty? My father hid and supported Cian for years, making sure that he wasn't killed or sent away to die again. He's a great man, and he loves me. I never loved you, and I certainly never loved Drake! As if I would lower myself to love a human!"

She slapped him again, and his head rocked with the force of it. He didn't realize how strong she was. The sting woke his senses. His skin prickled where she'd struck him. All the hurts on his body screamed out at once, making a bolt of pain slice through him from his head down to his feet.

"But that wasn't what I wished to speak to you about," Ailla turned and went to the bench along the wall, her hair floating behind her, and the sun lighting her from behind. "You wouldn't understand that, keeping to the purity of fae lines, of not allowing humans to dilute our blood and heritage."

Brennan remembered that Ailla had always been jealous of Iris.

"Why does that bother you so, if you have the man you desire?"

She didn't answer, still focused on what she was doing at the bench.

"Is it because you know that the human has something that you do not? In my case, the thing that made it impossible for me not to love her," he finished.

He knew this was a risk. He knew she was putting together something that would be painful and horrible if he couldn't get away. But he had to push her as much as he could.

She whirled around, clutching something in her hand and approached the table where he lay. "What, exactly, does your human have, Brennan? What is her irresistible quality? Please do share. That way, Cian and I know what to look for as we rip it from her," She grinned, and it was one of the evilest things he'd ever seen.

He realized she was doing the same thing to him that he attempted to do to her. But he knew that she would not lay hands on Iris. There was no way she could get to Iris. Not ever. He forced himself to breathe, to not become alarmed. It would lead him right into her trap.

"I will tell you, but you should be afraid. If she tempted me, what would she do to Cian? He has greater experience than I at keeping the interest of—" he stopped, deliberately. He wanted to see what she would do.

His words found their mark. "What are you talking about?" She screamed, gripping whatever she held in both hands now. "I am his only love; there is no one else!"

Brennan raised a brow. Ailla was not a fool. She must know that something with Cian was not right. She must have caught him in a lie at some point. A man couldn't maintain two lives for as long as Cian had without slips happening somewhere.

He took a breath and summoned his strength. He was fairly confident that she would try to kill him. He needed to ward himself as best he could before he spoke.

She took several steps towards him, and he braced himself for being hit once more.

"Really, Ailla? I've met a woman who is the daughter of the former Goblin King who has a differing opinion from you regarding Cian," he made himself smile as he spoke. "Perhaps you've met?"

A shift crossed Ailla's face as she held out the thing she'd been holding tightly. A small flask.

"This is nothing less than what you deserve," she breathed, coming closer.

Iris

*N*o one spoke. I didn't even want to breathe. There was another bang, and then a clatter as if someone dropped a bag of...who knew what? Something noisy.

A voice rang out. A language other than English, of course. Even without knowing what was said, I could hear the angry tone of the speaker. And frustration.

I would bet we'd found the staff of this joint. Having met Ailla, I'd bet they were not happy campers. Waiting on that bitch—she was the type who wanted hand-and-foot service.

Maybe they'd let us walk on by, handing us a sword as we went?

The thought made me want to giggle. But I didn't dare to make a sound.

Drake hugged the wall, and I felt Taranath come closer behind me. I leaned against the wall, noting that the warm hue of the castle stones was not the truth. They were cold to the touch.

"Be ready," Drake whispered. "Taranath, behind me," he added.

Taranath moved around me, stones in each hand. I caught his expression as he did do—never had I seen such fierceness on his face. He almost always looked placid and calm.

While I was still thinking about it, Drake and

Taranath moved together, almost as one. When did they get the time to practice like this? It looked more like a dance than a prelude to attack.

I held my own stones tightly in my hand, hands away from me slightly so that they were ready should I need them. In spite of the underlying anxiety for Brennan, I didn't want to do anything that would mess up whatever Drake and Taranath were planning to do.

The two of them slid around the corner, and I followed. I tried keeping a visual on what was going on in front of us by positioning myself in between the two of them. I was able to look between their shoulders. I could see three people beyond us, all of whom were wearing leather armor and had the look of soldiers. They were arguing, although not as loudly as the first voice we heard.

It happened in slow motion, almost like something you'd see in the movies. First one soldier saw us and then the other two turned around. It was apparent that they did not expect to see anyone here because they all stood frozen as if unsure what to do.

Abruptly, like glass shattering, the three soldiers came at us, two of them yelling. They spoke in the same language as before, so as usual, I had no idea what they said. Drake and Taranath rushed towards them. Drake swung his sword, and Taranath had his hands out in front of them. Without warning, a bright gold light shot from the mage's hands. Two of the three soldiers blasted back into the wall, their armor making a dull, thudding sound against the stones.

The third soldier had drawn his sword and faced off against Drake. Drake had a vicious grin on his face crouched low and circling, and he was muttering and what I thought was Fae. The soldier spat something back at him, and it sounded like he was spitting. Whatever he said made sense to Drake because I saw Drake's expression harden. A movement from the corner of my eye made me turn my head. I saw Taranath standing over the two soldiers who'd been blasted into the wall. Figuring that Drake had the third soldier under control, I sidled over next to Taranath.

"Will they live?" I asked.

"Yes, they will live. I don't intend to kill." Taranath looked at me his expression still severe and fierce. "But I hit them hard enough so that they won't wake up and bother us before we have to leave."

I nodded. "That makes sense, but—," we both turned to look as Drake and the soldier yelled at one another, and their swords clashed with the sound of metallic thunder. They were close enough that together their swords locked. The sound of metal was like grinding like nails on a chalkboard.

Instinctively, I moved closer to Taranath, the act of watching this life-and-death struggle making me scared. Drake was clearly the better warrior, but the soldier had at least 6 inches on him and was burly and muscled.

Drake pushed the soldier, who took two steps backward, stumbling. Drake didn't even hesitate. He stepped forward, sword at waist level, and ran the soldier through with his sword.

The air stilled. I could see the dust motes floating in the sunlight from the small windows in the stone above our heads. Clearly, the soldier was as surprised as the rest of us — well, at least me. He looked at Drake, his hands creeping to where the sword went through his belly. As he did so, his own sword clattered to the floor, the sound ringing throughout the court order.

Drake jerked his sword back towards himself, and it slid from the soldier noiselessly. The soldier looked down at his wound then back up at Drake and over at Taranath and I. Then, gracefully for such a large man, he crumpled to the floor.

"Oh my God," I breathed.

Drake leaned down, wiping his sword on the pant leg of the fallen soldier. "I'm surprised we've made it this far without getting into a fight," he said grimly. "Let's hope that was their primary source of protection."

He walked past the soldier he killed, and the two

that Taranath had thrown. He continued down the corridor as though this were no big deal.

Taranath followed him. Still looking at the scene of bodies, I trailed behind him. This entire journey, none of this seemed this real. But looking at the dead man and the two others, it hit home.

We could die here. Brennan could die here. We might not make it out alive.

I jumped as a hand landed on my shoulder.

"Iris, stop thinking like that." Taranath leaned close to me, making sure I met his eyes. "You are free to think like that once we're done, but such thoughts will not help us until after we have freed the King."

"You're right," I said softly still looking at the fallen men. "I know you're right. But..."

His arm went around me, and he pulled me away from the scene. "I know my lady," he said.

I turned my head and left the scene of destruction behind us. I hoped it would be the last. Unless, of course, we were able to wipe the floor with Cian and Ailla. Somehow, the thought of leaving them senseless or dead on the floor didn't seem as bothersome.

You know, because it was due to them that we were here. They were the ones who had stolen my husband, and they were the ones who were trying their best to ruin everything I cared about. Maybe I wasn't as fragile as I thought. But the soldiers didn't look evil, or horrible in any way. I assume they were from the Dragon Realm or at least attached to the Dragon Court. Which, in spite of my bias, didn't mean they were bad guys. I sighed as Taranath hurried us along behind Drake. This was not the time to get moral. This was the time to be fierce, and get Brennan back.

Then I'd have time to fall apart. Later.

Ahead of us, Drake stopped suddenly. He held out his hand, and mage and I stopped as well. I tried to breathe quietly as we listened.

And then I heard it. The voice of a woman, an angry woman. She wasn't quite shouting; she wasn't making any attempts to hide that she was angry and yelling.

A moment of silence and then to sounds rang out. Sharp, staccato, they were unmistakable.

The cracking sounds were those of one person slapping another.

We'd found Brennan.

15

Brennan

He eyed Ailla and the flask. "What is it you think you can do?" He put a laugh into his question. "Ailla, there's a reason that Cian hasn't let you participate. It's not because he's protecting you from me, or from the effects of magic." He met her eyes, and stared hard at her. "It's because you are not capable."

He'd either pushed her over the edge or gotten a lot closer to death. He hoped that Iris would be safe.

"You...." She started to swear at him in fae, but it was dragon-slang fae, earthy and crass. She unstopped the little flask, and wisps of smoke came out.

"This is less than you deserve, Brennan. For using me. For daring to replace me with that human!"

Ailla lifted the flask up. Brennan let out his breath, keeping his eyes on her. He would not flinch. He didn't doubt that whatever was in it would hurt, and make him miserable. But he'd survived worse than Ailla. Interesting that Iris still bothered her so. She hadn't wanted him, any more than he wanted her.

She tilted the little flask, and a few drops of the smoky liquid dropped onto his chest. It started to burn, and he could see smoke rising from him.

He closed his eyes. He didn't want her to see anything that might encourage her, or make her feel powerful. He concentrated on keeping the damage at the surface, although it was hard.

He could hear his skin sizzling.

Then the door to the room slammed open. He opened his eyes to see a streak of orange light shoot from the door right at Ailla.

Ailla stepped back when the door shot open, and when the light hit her, she slammed into the bench behind her. Glass and other things shattered as she fell. The flask she'd been holding over him dropped from her hands, adding to the noise. He couldn't see it, but it sounded like it went off with a bang.

He turned his head and saw Ailla push herself up and throw out her hand. As she did, another flash of light hit her, this time green. When she fell back, he could tell that she was hurt. She didn't get up.

Crunching of glass on the other side of him made him turn the other direction. The movement rippled across his chest, and searing pain ripped through him where the liquid had hit.

"Leave you alone for moments, and you end up here," Drake's voice said next to him.

Brennan was surprised to feel the beginning of tears in his eyes. He hadn't cried since he was a child. He opened his mouth, but couldn't speak because Drake was shoved unceremoniously out of the way, and Iris cupped his face with her hands.

Tears streamed down her face. Better that way, better that she cry for both of them he thought.

She kissed him, and said something, but he couldn't understand her.

"Your Majesties, we must go," the voice of Taranath said behind Iris.

Brennan felt the bindings that held him to the table releasing. He had known they must have been held in place with magic—but it was good to know that his mage was capable of dismantling them.

"I am not sure I will be able to walk," he said, between Iris kissing him. "I have not been allowed to move from here since they took me."

"Well, at least they didn't kill you," Drake said, still obscenely cheerful.

It was not for a lack of trying," said Brennan. "Actually, now that I think of it, Cian wasn't ready to kill me. Ailla would have ended my life some time ago. If she'd been given the chance."

"Those assholes," Iris stood back, and marched around the table to where Ailla lay on the bench. "You crazy bitch. What are we going to do with her?" The disgust in her voice was apparent.

"We are going to leave her, and get out of here before anyone else comes around," Drake said. "Lordship, you're going to need to let me carry you. I can't have you slowing us down, old man." He grinned.

"I'll never hear the end of this, will I?" Brennan asked. His voice sounded hoarse to his ears, and he felt more tired than he'd been in ages. The room was crowded with the extra people, and as Drake carefully lifted him from the table into a sitting position, he could feel the unused muscles protesting.

"Probably not," Drake said cheerfully, "But I'll let some time pass before I bring it up."

"Let's not waste any time," Taranath said. "Majesty, if you would help me, we'll get a portal opened."

With a final withering glance at the prone Ailla, Iris walked around the table and joined Taranath. He handed her a stone, and took her hand in his.

What had Cian and Ailla said? That there were people in the Goblin Realm—

"Wait!" He held up a hand, amazed at the effort the simple gesture took.

Iris and Taranath looked up.

"We cannot go to the Goblin Castle. They told me they had allies there. We need to go to the Fae Castle and warn Father and Mother."

"Jharak is at the Goblin Castle," Iris said. "I think he's hiding out from Nerida at the moment."

Drake chuckled, but Brennan's stomach churned in worry. His parents not together, and not of one mind— it was one more way to divide the Realms.

"We have to get to Fae Castle," he said again. "Send Father a message, and tell him to meet us there."

"That leaves our home undefended!" Iris exclaimed.

"Our home is merely a stopping point on the path of a worse plan," Brennan said. "It's not just me that they are after. Cian's goals include taking over the entire Realm. And why is Father in my Castle?"

"Because Mother is on a tear, doesn't want any of us hurting her precious baby boy," Drake said, the sarcasm dripping from his tone. "She made it very clear that she was not happy we were going on a mission to save you and kill Cian."

"I still can't understand that," Iris interjected. "Yes he's her son too, but he's trying to hurt you."

"It's not that simple," Taranath interjected.

"I don't care how tough it is! I can certainly understand wanting to deal with brother, but only after you get the kidnapped son back!" Iris had her hands on her hips.

Brennan couldn't believe the surge of love that he felt watching her. To have someone other than Drake so loyal, so fierce in his defense was something new. For years he'd carried the burden of his brother's death. And now he knew it was all false. A lie. A burden that he did not have carried. Watching Iris defend him warmed his heart in ways he didn't think was possible.

A movement at his shoulder made him turn his head. Drake was watching him watch Iris.

"She's done very well," said Drake quietly. "She never gave up on you."

"Would you have let her?" Brennan asked.

"Never," Drake said firmly. "But that wouldn't even be a question with her."

Brennan knew it for the accolade it was. A part of him couldn't wait to hear how they managed to find their way here.

"As fascinating as this is, we do really need to leave." Drake was all business. "Your ladyship? As much as I enjoy watching your temper tantrum, we don't have the time or the luxury for this."

Drake's snide words were designed to goad Iris into action. It worked.

"Well then, I don't know why you're still standing here! Let's go!"

Mage moved to the door, opening it carefully, and sticking his head out.

"Wait!" Brennan held up a hand again.

"What now?" Drake asked.

Brennan didn't imagine the annoyance in Drake's tone. "One of the reasons that I didn't die was because of someone who helped me here. A woman called Aine." He looked at Drake, hoping he remembered the significance of the name. "I promised her I take her with me when I escaped. She knew you would come for me. I can't go back on my word."

Iris stepped towards him, her hand still on her hips. "Who is Aine?"

A dead man could've heard the menace in her words. He remembered her anger over the spy in the Dragon Court. While he felt certain that had been a part of Ailla's spell, he didn't want to give her any cause for jealousy.

"She saved my life. I'm not exactly sure she is, or why she wishes to leave so desperately, but as she does,

and I owe her she will come with us. We must
find her."

"We really are pressed for time," Taranath said.

"I'm not abandoning someone who risks their life
to help me," Brennan said, glaring around at the other
three. "The Goblin King does not go back on his word."

Iris

I couldn't believe him. After everything we
done to get here, after all that we had risk,
and now he was going to hold up the show waiting on
some woman? Why was it always some woman when it
came to Brennan? Why was I still worry about this?
After all, I was married to him.

I was married to him. He had all this time to find
someone else, and yet he married me. I had to
remember that, but my jealousy and insecurity got the
better of me. I had been — and was — Brennan's
choice. If he said he'd given this word because this
woman had helped him, then that is what it was. He
given his word. He would not be a man I loved if he
failed to keep his word.

"No, he does not." I said smiling Brennan. "So let's
find this chick, and get out here before sleeping ugly
wakes up." I jerked my chin in the direction of Ailla.

Her breathing had become heavy. I had to be honest — it would make my day if she started to snore.

Drake and Taranath both smiled at my description of Ailla. While physically she was beautiful, I couldn't look at her without seeing ugly that lay within. If that made me sound like the jealous wife, so be it.

"Where would she be, Brennan?" I asked.

"I'm not sure," he said shaking his head. "She has always just sort of shown up."

Drake made a noise of disgust. "Very helpful, Lordship."

"I am deeply sorry to disappoint you. One takes friends where one can find them."

"Especially in this dump," I muttered.

Taranath patted me on the shoulder. I thought he might be able to feel my anger rising. I had a hard enough time with control when I wasn't mad or scared; I didn't need to make things worse.

I saw Brennan notice the gesture, but his face remained blank. That meant he would ask me about it later. It made me smile, and some of my anger ease, to think that I'd be able to tell him not only how I'd grown magically, but how his two chief advisors and I had become closer, more a team.

I hoped he'd be pleased. He'd ruled alone for a long time.

He chose me. I had to remember that. He chose

me. I shook my head, wanting to dispel that nasty voice of doubt within. I hated it, but if I ignored it, rather than banishing it, it would sit and fester, getting louder and more insistent every time I allowed it to surface. Ailla's spell had shown me that.

Speaking of which...I looked over to where she lay, still unconscious on the table, tossed into all the crap on it like a used piece of tissue.

Then I looked at Brennan, and saw how gaunt, how pale he looked. For the first time since I'd met him, he looked every one of his six hundred and seventy four years.

Ailla had done this. Cian had done this. I remembered my vow back at the Castle, in my home. I would kill them both.

I moved swiftly, taking a stone from my pocket. Taranath and Brennan saw me, but Taranath got there first. Brennan was still supported by Drake. Damn that bitch straight to hell.

And this room—this was where they'd kept him? Poky, airless little place, more like a walk-in closet. There was a window, but it didn't look like it had been opened in centuries.

The smell was one of despair, and taking all this in, my anger went white hot.

"No, Iris, you cannot." Taranath's voice was calm in my ear.

I shrugged off his arm. "She's our enemy. She tried to kill our king—my husband! She needs to go. Like, right now!"

"Iris, love," Brennan said quietly. "We cannot kill her. We have enough challenges as it is. If she is going to die, it has to be after the entire Realm—all the Realms—hear what she has done. What she and Cian and Eilor have done. They will be executed humanely."

"But—" I protested.

He put a hand on my face, and drew me close. "We are not them," he said.

That did it for me. He was right. We were not them. We didn't give into anger, or hate, or any of that crap when we acted. We weren't animals. She and Cian— they were. I put my arms around his neck, and held him to me, ignoring the smell. Ewww. They hadn't even bothered to toss water on him while he was here.

I couldn't think about that, or I'd get mad all over again.

"Will you come to the other side and help me?" Brennan whispered into my hair. "I don't want to ask anyone else for help."

The thought that he would lean on me before the guys—warmed me to my core. He wasn't afraid that I would see him as a person. Well, a Fae person. Because he loved me, and I loved him.

Any more of this crazed emotion see saw, and I'd be crying like a baby. Not pretty crying either. Ugly, snot-nosed, red-faced sobbing.

"Yeah. Thank god we found you," I whispered back. Another quick hug, and then I let go of him and walked to the other side of the table, close to sleeping ugly.

Could she just snore or make some unpleasant bodily noise? Just something so that she didn't lay there looking all beautiful? For Pete's sake. I wanted to see one thing that brought her down to size.

Apparently, I hadn't gotten past all the snubs she'd tossed at me before. I mentally shrugged. Some people, you didn't get past it. Ailla would be one of those people for me. I edged around her, and got my arm around Brennan's waist.

With Drake's help, and me supporting him, we helped him to slide off the table. He stumbled forward as Drake caught him.

Yeah, they were totally going to die for this. I didn't care what it took.

"I'm going to need to put you over my shoulder," Drake said to Brennan leaning back as he supported him.

Brennan side. "If you must," he said wearily.

Drake left, just a little bit. "You'll thank me, when we use the escape route out here."

I rolled my eyes "Oh my God. We have to go back out the same way we came in?" I couldn't believe it. We have to go through that stinky, smelly, tunnel again? Gross.

"Unless you have a better idea, ladyship," Drake said. "Disgusting, yes. Easy, and undetectable? Yes."

I groaned, but didn't say anything else. His words made sense. I just didn't want to hear it. Or admit it.

Taryn if, who had been holding out the door, peered out and then turned back to the three of us. "We should probably go there's no one about, but we don't know how many more there are. Were you given any sense of how many staff might be here, your Majesty?" This was directed at Brennan.

Brennan shook his head. "This was the only part of the Castle I've seen. They didn't let me out of here."

I narrowed my eyes and breathe deeply through my nose. I was right. They hadn't let him out, hadn't let him use the bathroom, and hadn't even bothered to throw a damn bucket of water on him. Yeah, I was going to push hard for a swift and public execution.

Drake picked up Brennan and hoisted him onto his shoulders. He grunted a little with the weight, but then stood up straight and got a better hold on Brennan.

"I'm just not sure this could get any less dignified," Brennan grumbled.

It thrilled me that he sounded like his old self. Just for that one moment. But I take it.

Taranath stood back, so that Drake could get out the door with Brennan. I put my hand on the door next to him, and said "Go on. I'll close the door. Better that they think he still in here."

Taranath nodded and walked through the doorway.

At that moment, I heard the tinkling of glass I looked over my shoulder, and there was Ailla, struggling to sit up. She had almost pushed herself into a sitting position, and there was murder written all over her.

"You," she hissed. Sounding just like the snake she was.

I didn't think I didn't even think my thoughts through. In four short strides, I'd made it around the table and just as she was raising her arm, I drew back mine.

Bam!

My fist connected with her nose. Blood spurted as though from a geyser, spring me in the face.

She opened her mouth, and I hit her in the nose again. *Bam!*

She looked at me, and then her eyes glossed over. It was that look I called the glazed doughnut. When you can see that someone totally checks out on you.

Usually, I saw when I went on too long talking about sailing.

Thankfully, however, Ailla went glazed doughnut on me because I'd knocked her right in the kisser.

"Iris! Are you all right?" Taranath had come back in, his hand out, ready to do whatever was needed. Even Drake had come back and peered in through the doorway. I could see Brennan's worried face in the background.

I turned around, a smile on my features as I wiped my bloodied hand on that dumb bitch's dress.

"I'm fine. Never felt better. Just taking care of little last-minute problem. Get the hell out of here."

As I walked towards the door, Drake started to laugh. "Did you really just punch her in the nose?"

I nodded, the grin spreading wide across my face. "Damn right. It's the very least I could do."

A moment of silence greeted my words, and then all three of them started to laugh.

"Be quiet!" I hissed, looking around nervously. As good as it felt to hit Ailla, we were out of the woods yet. "We need to get out of here! Let's find Aine, and get back in the stinky tunnel."

We hadn't taken more than four steps down the hallway when Taranath pushed his way in front of Drake and I, hand out.

I could almost feel the energy radiating from him,

and wondered what it was that he saw that we hadn't seen yet.

Taranath's actions spurred on Drake. He crouched down, and set Brennan up against the wall. "Iris, watch him. Get out one your stones." Without waiting to see if I did so, he turned and stood shoulder to shoulder with mage.

The moment felt heavy, pregnant with waiting. No one moved. I was afraid to breathe. And then everything happened quickly.

Drake lunged forward, sword in hand. Taranath was right next to him, energy crackling around his hand in the stony health.

I had my arm around Brennan, but I couldn't take my eyes off of the scene in front of me. I hope to be able to get spell out, and do it right. This wasn't the time to screw things up.

Brennan must have been watching the scene in front of us as well, because suddenly he half shouted, "Wait!"

His words stilled the other men, but neither put down their weapons. Brennan pushed himself off the wall, with an arm around my shoulders for support. He took a few steps forward, coming to stand in between the shoulders of Drake and Taranath.

"Aine? Is that you?"

As if from thin air, the head, and then the body of a

dark-haired girl, not much older than me, appeared. Those were some skills I needed to learn. Add more to the list of things I needed to learn. I hoped this was Aine, so I can answer ask her to teach me.

"Were you leaving me?" Her voice was low, and I could hear the potential for anger in it.

"We were looking for you," Brennan answered quickly. His voice sounded strong, with no doubt whatsoever. "Where did you go, when Ailla came in?"

Aine shrugged. "I'd be dead if I didn't have ways to get away from her," she said, her voice still quiet.

I got the impression she didn't speak loudly.

Her words fell like rocks falling from the sky. The weight of them was heavy, and it made me wish I'd punched her one more time.

Drake was not one to be struck by the sentimentality of the situation. "Can you get us out of here?" He asked. As he spoke, he came back he turned around and shouldered Brennan once more.

Aine eyed first Drake, and then Brennan. "Interesting," was all she said.

I almost wanted to laugh. I was afraid, however, that either Brennan or Drake would kill me. I really hope she was friendly, because I could tell already that I was going to like her great deal. She didn't take anything from anyone. And anyone who could escape Ailla with regularity was definitely worth knowing.

I pushed past Drake and Taranath and held out my hand. "I'm Iris. Brennan's told us of what you did for him. I can't thank you enough. Can you please show us how to get out of here? The sooner we do, the sooner we can get to the Fae Castle."

Her dark eyes looked me up and down. I felt as though I was being judged, weighed, and measured. She looked young, but her eyes spoke of an old soul. Maybe just someone who'd been through a lot. I was going to guess that it was the latter rather than the former.

"You have blood all over you," she said quietly.

I grinned. "Courtesy of Ailla," I said with great satisfaction.

Her eyebrows rose. "Did you kill her?"

"No, he wouldn't let me." I jerked my head back towards Brennan "Apparently, we'll get to see her die in front of the entire Fae court."

She took my hand, and squeezed it. "I want to see that," she said.

"Done." I said.

Drake cleared his throat. "Are we done, ladies? Can we please get moving before more guards come to stop us?"

Aine shot an unfathomable look at Drake, and then turned. She didn't speak, nor did we. We followed her and I marveled at how quiet and sure she was. Her footsteps, her stance, everything about her spoke of stealth and moving carefully. It was really very impressive to watch. I could see now, with no jealousy or any other negative feelings, why Brennan had agreed to bring her with him. This woman would be a strong ally.

Almost as though she could read my thoughts, she whipped her head over her shoulder to glance at me. I smiled, and she smiled back. Just a small smile. I knew, right then, I'd made a friend. All on my own, and not because I was married to Brennan.

"Um, Aine? Anyway we could skip that disgusting tunnel?"

A noise that might have been a laugh came from her. "There is another way," she said. Her stride didn't slow down at all.

Thankfully, we didn't see anyone else. In my concern over Brennan, I'd forgotten that brother was probably in the castle as well.

Again, as though someone read my thoughts, I heard a shout from the direction that we come from.

Apparently someone had discovered Ailla.

Brennan

$\mathcal{A}$s they followed behind Aine, Brennan worried. Not just because he was being jogged along on Drake's shoulders, but because he hoped they would get to the Fae Castle in time. If what Drake said was true, his father waited for them in the Goblin Castle. That left his mother all alone. And from the little Drake had said, she wouldn't see Cian as an enemy. She see him as her long-lost son.

Again, ignoring the inglorious manner in which he was being transported, he couldn't believe how happy he was. Aine had been convinced that his family would come to get him. He'd hoped she was right, but deep inside he wasn't sure. He hadn't been sure they would get to him on time. Now that he was leaving this place, he admitted to himself that he'd been worried that Cian would kill him before his family found him.

Yet here they were. And they had come through something—he couldn't tell what it was—but Iris, Drake, and Taranath were a team. If he were a lesser man, he would feel a bit jealous.

But he didn't. Instead, he was thrilled his wife, the only other person he loved as much as he loved Drake, was now part of their team.

As he bounced up and down on Drake's shoulder, Brennan considered all of this, hopefully in an attempt to ignore the pain in his midsection from Drake's shoulder. He did not regret marrying Iris. It was the best thing he had ever done for himself. But nor would he lie to himself about his worry and fears as to how she would fit into his world. He knew the way his people looked at humans. Drake had proven himself hundreds of times over, and yet there were still those who would not accept him as a potential air to the Fae throne.

Not that Drake wanted the throne. He'd been pretty clear about that.

Drake stopped abruptly, and Brennan felt the shoulder gouge deep in his gut. He wanted to moan, but he wasn't going to. He was just happy to be out of that room. A bit more pain wasn't going to kill him. He laughed to himself at his dark humor. He considered sharing it, but didn't think his companions would find it as funny as he did.

Aine had reached a door, and she opened it and peered carefully around it. She turned back towards the rest of them. "All right, it's clear. We can go."

Drake didn't move. "Where, exactly are we going?"

Taranath stepped in here. "We need to portal to the Fae Castle."

"But I thought we were trying to avoid magical detection?" Iris looked from one to the other. "Isn't that why I have a sore butt from a horse? Or has that now completely gone out the window?"

"We don't have time for that anymore. If Brennan's right, and they're headed for the Fae Castle, Father is still at the Goblin Castle. That leaves Mother on her own."

As usual, Drake's thinking ran with his own. He didn't even have to say anything. Drake saw the problems from the moment Brennan told him what he knew.

Iris peered out the door over Aine's shoulder. "You're sure no one will see us?"

Aine shook her head. "They didn't keep very many guards or staff here. Ailla complained because she had to help the cooking."

Iris actually laughed out loud. "Oh, I bet she was real happy,"

Aine shot her a rare smile, and nodded. "I hid for three days after that," she said.

Drake made an impatient noise, and pushed past the two women. He strode out into the open area, stopping to turn and call quietly over his shoulder "Taranath, can you get us there?"

Taranath followed Drake, digging into his pouch as he did so. Brennan saw all this by looking back from Drake shoulders. It felt odd to see all this, but not be an active part. He wanted to—it didn't matter what he wanted right now. He was better not being in the way.

Taranath said, "Yes. I think this is a big enough space, I'll need to open up a fairly large portal. In order to get all of us in weekly." Drake stopped

Drake stopped and turned around, momentarily blocking Brennan's vision. He adjusted himself on Drake shoulder so he could watch what was going on. It galled him to not be in charge, but he knew he would be more of a hindrance than a help. He was so weak, he would just have to sit with his injured pride.

Taranath murmured something, and a faint blue light began to glow. A small circle at first, and then larger as he continued to speak, everyone watched quietly as the portal got bigger and bigger.

Taranath stopped speaking the spell and turned

towards everyone else. "I believe this is big enough," he said. Drake took one step towards the portal, but Iris held out her hand.

"Are we sure this is the Fae Castle?" she asked.

Drake snorted. "Taranath is doing the portal, not you, ladyship," he said.

So quickly that Brennan was sure he didn't see it, Iris reached out and slapped Drake on the shoulder. "You're supposed to be nice to the people who are learning!"

"Nice ended with you dropping us in the troll dungeon," Drake snapped back.

"Really, if we could all just go through the portal, that would move things along much more quickly," Taranath said.

Brennan covered his mouth so that he didn't laugh out loud. Iris and Drake bickered like a brother and sister. And she dropped them in a troll dungeon? That was one story he would need to hear. Later, maybe. After he'd gotten a bath, and some sleep. And he wouldn't be angry at Iris for putting herself at risk. He promised himself that he wouldn't yell at her. She had only done what he would have.

He stopped those thoughts. The two men he trusted most other than his father had been with her. They'd kept her safe. For that, he would be forever grateful.

He closed his eyes and sense words of thanks towards the stars that his family, thus far, was safe. As they stepped through the portal, he could feel some of the tension fall off of his body.

They had made it. They were in his Father's home.

Now, all he needed to do was face his mother. If she was still safe. And alive.

Iris

For once, I was glad I hadn't been doing the driving. Taranath had done a good job, dropping us what looked like right in the dining room. How did he get so specific? I added learning that to the ever growing list of things I needed to know.

If it wasn't the dining room, it was somewhere equally big and grand. Wherever it was, we were in the right place. Jharak and Nerida stood there, staring at us as though we grown three heads each. It was obvious they'd been arguing.

Nerida recovered first. "What are you all doing here?" she asked, disbelief in her voice. "Oh my goodness! Drake — Brennan — oh my goodness! What has happened to you?"

I stepped forward. "Your son, Cian, and Ailla happened." My voice was flat, and I couldn't keep the anger from it. "This is his handiwork. Their handiwork. They did this! Look at your son, Nerida! Your other son, the one you're busy crying over, he did this!"

While I'd been speaking, Drake had knelt down and put Brennan on his feet. He stood him right next to me, and Brennan put one arm around my waist. As weak as he was, his presence steadied me. He was here. He was with me. He was alive. I opened my mouth to speak again, and he put his other hand on the shoulder closest to him. I stopped.

"Mother, we need to prepare. Cian and Ailla plan to come here, and dispose of the two of you." His stark words dropped into the room like rain on a parade. Nerida and Jharak both stared at him, mouths slightly agape.

"Brennan, you've obviously been hurt, and had a very difficult time," Nerida said, her voice slightly patronizing.

It made me want to punch her the same way I punched Ailla.

Drake obviously felt the same way. "No, Mother, it's not just that he's had a hard time. He's been tortured, they've been draining him." Brennan turned to look at his brother so quickly I thought he give himself whiplash. I didn't remember him saying that. How did Drake know?

Drake glanced at Brennan, and their eyes met. Something passed between them, but I didn't have a good enough angle to see exactly what it was. Drake turned back to his mother.

"They were going to kill him. That was their plan. Which is why they weren't afraid to tell him what they were planning. Cian never planned to let Brennan leave alive, no matter what lies he told you!" Drake stopped, breathing deeply.

It was nice to see I wasn't the only one about to lose my temper with Nerida.

Drake continued, "Aine told Brennan that they were going first to the Goblin Castle, and then they were coming here. Just like they were planning to kill Brennan, they were going to kill the two of you. Yes, Mother, that includes you. So before you go crying for your poor lost son, perhaps you should consider that."

Nerida didn't take this sort of abuse lying down. I knew she was going to blow the moment that Drake started speaking. "How dare you speak to me so, Drake? What do you know of Cian? What do any of you know of Cian? I am his mother! I know my son!" In that moment, I wasn't sure that Nerida was safe from any of us. Her blatant refusal, her complete denial — I know it had to make everybody else as crazy as it made me.

But before anyone could punch the queen in the nose, Aine step forward.

"Your Majesty," Aine dropped almost to a knee, in some weird parity of a curtsy and a bow. "My name is Aine. I have grown up in the Dragon Court. I knew your son, although not as Cian. I knew him as Kelan. Your son Drake speaks the truth. I have heard Cian and Ailla speak of their plans. Plans they made along with Eilor."

Nerida held up a hand, stopping Aine from speaking further. "And just who are you? I don't know you. I don't know that anything you say is true."

I took several steps forward to stand next to Aine. "This woman is the only reason that your oldest son, Brennan, is alive! She made sure to go in and heal him after Psycho One and Psycho Two had their fun with him! Can't you see him?" I turned around and gestured at Brennan. "Does he look good to you? Does he look healthy? Or does he look worn, and tired, and tortured? Are you blind, or just trying to be stupid?"

You could've dropped a rock in the silence that followed my question. I almost clapped my hand over my mouth, but then decided the hell with it. Nerida needed to hear the truth. If she was going to stand here and deny what we can all see with our own eyes, and she was going to have to face that lie head-on. And own it. I wasn't going to cut her any further slack.

"You stay out of this young lady!" Nerida shook her finger at me. "You have even less idea than anyone else of what is going on!"

At this point that Jharak came up, and put his arms around Nerida's shoulders. "Nerida, why don't we have Brennan seen to? And allow the others, who also look tired and done in, to rest and refresh themselves? Then we can all speak together again." While his words were gentle, his tone was firm. There would be no arguing.

Brennan's hand reached for mine, giving it a squeeze. I knew that squeeze. It meant, *Shut up, Iris. You've said enough.* Even though I was sure Brennan would never say *Shut up* to me.

Nerida looked at him, anger warring the desire to tear into us further. Then she looked at us, and made a disgusted noise. She whirled around, her skirts flaring out she did so and walked to the other end of the large dining. Without a backwards glance, without another word, she opened the door and walked through it. She slammed it behind her.

"Well, that went well." Drake looked at his father.

Jharak didn't answer, but came straight to Brennan. "What did they do to you?"

Whatever Nerida believed, it was obvious that Jharak believed us.

Brennan tried to laugh, but ended up coughing. "What didn't they do, Father?" He asked. "What they were trying to do, and doing a decent job of it, was drain me of all of my magic."

The sound of him nearly broke my heart, and hardened it further towards Cian and Ailla.

Jharak's brow furrowed as he thought about this. "Why were they trying to drain you of your magic?"

Brennan shrugged. "I don't know. I've never heard of stealing someone else's magical ability. But Cian is crazy, Father. You need to know that. He is truly, absolutely, crazy. There is no reasoning with him. He lived for years in the Dragon Court, and whatever happened there, has made him lose touch with what is real. He was always mean, as a child," Brennan looked off in the distance, and I could tell that he was remembering.

"After I was declared the heir to the Goblin Realm, we were no longer brothers in his eyes. He's kept that hurt open, and alive. It's like a wound it's never been allowed to heal." Brennan looked at his father and put the hand that had been resting on my shoulder on Jharak's arm.

"Father, he cannot be allowed to live. There is no way that allowing him to live will give us the peace that I know you wish for." He stared into his father's eyes as he spoke, and I knew he was trying to tell his dad that they were going to have to kill Cian.

At this point, I wish I had the magical ability to do

it myself. Because I didn't have any problem killing the guy. Or Ailla. Or crazy dad. All three of them deserve death. Preferably, a slow, painful death.

But I knew my Brennan, and I knew his father. I knew they would make sure that all three of these terrible, traitorous, dangerous people were put to death humanely, and cleanly.

In my opinion, it couldn't be too soon.

Jharak stared at Brennan, looking him over carefully. "You look terrible, my son. Let's go get you tended to, and then we'll take care of Cian."

How did he do it? Dad was so calm, so gentle with his words, but you could feel the strength behind them. I knew then, no matter what, Cian was going to die.

I just hope *we* all made it through.

17

Brennan

*B*rennan felt his heart race, and he pushed himself up. He was not in his room at the castle. Well, he was in his room. But his old room in the Fae Castle, not the Goblin Castle. He looked over. Iris was not there. She had been there, the night before, after they'd bathed and had attended to his various wounds.

Taranath also given him a potion to help with the healing from a magical side of things. Quietly, major told him that he didn't think the damage was permanent. For that, Brennan was extremely thankful. It wasn't just the loss of magic. It was a loss of magic to Cian. It made him feel that Cian

had won something. That was the bitterest part
of all.

His head turned, listening. Something…something
was happening. Whatever it was, they had all gone to
deal with it. He didn't know how he knew, but he knew.
And he lived long enough to know that he did not
ignore his gut feelings. He threw his feet over the side
of the bed, and taking a deep breath pushed himself
up. He found that unlike yesterday, he could stand.
Taking his time, trying not to panic it how long this
was taking, he got himself dressed.

Someone, probably Drake, had left the sword by
the door. He took it up, feeling better with the heft of it
in his hand. Brennan stepped outside his room door
and stood for a moment. He wanted to see where his
instinct took him.

Where would they be? And why would they leave
him? A part of him was furious, even though he knew
they had done it for his own good. He could almost
hear Iris's voice in his head. *We just got you back! I'm not
going to lose you again!*

She might have said something like that the night
before. Right before he'd fallen asleep on her shoulder.
He been so tired, that's all he could do when finally
reunited with his wife. Fall asleep on her shoulder.
Well, things would be different tonight. As long as he
could find where it was the something was happening.

He stopped. He could hear voices — they were coming from the great hall. He made the turn down the corridor towards the great hall, picking up his pace as he did so.

Brennan was not surprised that there would be shouting and carrying on. Cian just couldn't do the thing, and be done with it. He knew, from talking to Cian all the time when he was trapped in the room, that Cian had an ax to grind. He wanted to be heard. He wanted to be...what was Iris's word? Validated?

Yes, that was it. Cian wanted to be validated. Right before he killed everyone that he claimed to love. Well, loved at one time. Brennan was pretty sure that Cian didn't love anyone anymore, no matter what he said.

As he got closer to the great hall, he could hear the voices rising. He stopped again, to catch his breath, and to listen. Yes, there was. He could hear Cian's voice. And then — Ailla's laugh. Cian must've fixed her nose.

He snickered at the thought. He wished he could have seen it, Iris hitting Ailla right in the face. Blood spurting everywhere. It must have been glorious! Perhaps he could talk to Taranath and see if they could review the memory somehow—he stopped himself. *Not the time, Brennan.*

When he reached the door, he noted that it was cracked open. Stepping carefully, he put his eye against the crack, and slowly, slowly pulled the door open just a little wider.

It was enough.

He could see Cian, with Ailla at his side. Cian had cast some sort of spell, similar to the spell that he had cast in the courtyard of the Goblin Castle several weeks before. It rose up to the top of the great hall, almost acting as a barrier between himself and Ailla and the rest of his family.

Brennan glanced around the hall. There were no guards, only his family. Drake and Jharak stood opposite brother, swords drawn.

Nerida stood off to one side, her hand to her mouth. Iris, Aine, and Taranath were on the other side of Drake and Father, and Iris and Aine looked as though they were ready to kill. Particularly Iris.

He smiled, feeling the warmth of her love and his pride in her suffuse through him. No wonder he had to wait for so long for her. She was magnificent in her anger.

He edged in through the door, taking care to hold his sword close so that it may no noise.

As expected, Cian was in the middle of some foolish, blowhard speech.

"You never loved me," Cian sneered, glancing between Nerida and Jharak. "Nanny Margot told me all about it. She told me you were glad that I was gone.

Glad to have me out of the way, so that you could focus on the precious Goblin King to be!"

"No!" wailed Nerida. "Cian, no! I cried for you! Many, many nights, I cried for you! We were told that you had died in the fire! We searched through all of the rubble, and the ashes! I searched myself! I was covered in ashes, fearing that they were the ashes of my son, and hoping that they were not! But there was no sign of you, or Margot! What else are we to think?"

Listening to his mother, Brennan actually felt pity for her. The emotion in her voice was real. In that moment, he could understand why she could not bear the thought of seeing Cian put down. She had never gotten over the loss of him. She'd never allowed herself to mourn, and was not able to let him go now that she thought she might have him back.

His heart hardened, as he thought of what brother had in store for all of them. He would just have to deal with the anger of his mother. It might take centuries, but as long as he had Father, and Drake, and his Iris, he would be all right.

Eventually, Nerida would see that there had been no other choice. He edged along the wall, attempting to come around and get closer to Cian, without anyone noticing.

As he watched the scene in front of him, he could tell that Drake and Father saw him. He didn't think that anyone would've noticed the slight start the Drake gave. No one else had fought with Drake like he had.

"Then why did you not search high and low for your son when you thought he had died?" Ailla asked. "Were it not for my father and me, he would have died."

Nerida was taking no nonsense from anyone, certainly not Ailla. Not even while facing down a magic that Brennan didn't even understand. He felt pride at his mother's strength. No matter how misplaced it was, there was no doubt as to her courage.

"I searched the entire Realm, and all the other Realms. Why did you and your father hide my son from me?" She took a few steps closer to Cian and Ailla and the glowing, protective magic that lay between them.

"Because my father knew, he knew! He knew what your plans were, and he didn't want to see the rightful heir to the throne put down!"

Brennan could see that this confrontation was going to go badly in a very short amount of time. He could feel the rising tension in the hall, feel the strength of the anger and all the emotions of the people within. He needed to get to Cian fast. Before someone was killed.

"Why, you arrogant—" Nerida took a few more

steps, and without warning, Cian directed the magic at her.

Whatever the magic was, it jumped from where it had been hovering in front of Cian, and struck Nerida. She fell backwards, and quick as lightning, Aine ran to her.

Drake and Jharak made a move as Nerida fell, but when they saw that Aine had gone to her they turned back towards Cian. Swords went higher, and Brennan could see that Taranath and Iris were advancing closer. Both held stones in their hands.

It would be long. He still wasn't close enough. Even if he was, he didn't have a stone. He would need to do this with sword alone. While he didn't want to admit it, he wasn't sure he was going to be able to defeat Cian.

But he could not leave him here with his family. Even if he had to die, he had to take Cian with him. Everyone else could take care of Ailla. He had to kill brother. The world slowed around him. Every movement sharpened. His heartbeat whispered in his ears, and he found his breath drawing deeper. Even if he died, he would take Cian with him.

Cian laughed as Nerida fell. "At long last, Mother," he sneered, putting special emphasis on the word mother, "you pay the price for your mistake, for your crime."

"Crime?" Asked Jharak. "Where is the crime in

mourning a lost child?"

"There was no mourning," said Cian. "Only lies! Lies, always lies! All you ever did was lie to me! Why would you tell the truth to the rest of the Realm? If you couldn't even tell your own son the truth?"

"So you admit, you are my son?" asked Jharak.

"I admit that at one point, I was your son," said Cian. His voice sounded dead, flat. "I am your son no longer. However, I will be when I should have always been. After tonight, I will be the Fae King. There's nothing you can do to stop it." The flat tone in which he delivered those last words struck Brennan.

Iris and Taranath had advanced a few more steps. They were almost directly behind Drake and father. Brennan could feel the hum of the energy as they both began to work their spells. *Just a little more time*, he thought. *I just need a little more time.*

Iris

I could see Brennan creeping along the far wall, trying to be quiet, trying to stay as close to invisible as he could. Cian was so busy proving his point; he didn't even bother to look around.

Cian could do some pretty crazy magic, but he wasn't much of a warrior. In just a short time that I'd been listening to him blather on, I could tell that in some ways, he never grown up. He was still that little boy, so angry, so offended, so sure that the entire world had done him wrong. How old was he now? He must be over seven-hundred years old, but he was going on about things that were ancient history? Things seen from the eyes of a kid?

And there was Ailla, staring at him as though he were the second coming. What she saw in him, I didn't know. Maybe crazy was attracted to crazy. Every now and again, she would look over and when her eyes met mine, hers shot hate daggers. I knew that I would have to be ready. She was going to come straight for me. Not just because I'd broken her nose. And I was pretty sure I broke it, even if magic had made it better. But because she was still angry with Brennan. Which was weird as she didn't want him anyway.

Guess there's no greater evil than a woman scorned. Even when that woman doesn't give two hoots about the man.

I looked over to see Aine working over Nerida. Thankfully, Nerida seem to be moving on her own, although not fully. At least she wasn't dead. I wondered if this would finally opened her eyes to what her precious baby boy had become.

A movement from Taranath next to me brought my attention back to the two nutballs. Time to focus. I held out my hands, each clutching a stone. I concentrated on Ailla. I needed to hit her first—no matter what. After that...I didn't know.

Whatever was going to happen, it was going to be soon. I could see — I could feel — the magic ramping up. It was almost as if electricity was gathering in the room.

The stones of the walls almost felt as though they were shivering and shuddering under the force of all the magic that was contained within this room. There was a breeze, even though none of the windows were open. And I knew it was from all the magic. Not only whatever crazy business Cian was doing, but from Taranath and myself. I was pretty certain that Drake and Jharak had something magical going on as well, but I couldn't be sure.

It felt as though there were a thousand bees humming in my ear. That's how I could tell. It was going to happen soon.

Cian opened his mouth, but whatever he was going to say was cut off by the glowing circle of a portal forming over to the left of us.

It felt as though time stopped in that moment, as we all turned and watched the portal. Small at first, light pink and blue in nature, and then it grew and grew until it was the size of a person.

It was very bright, and while I could see what

looked like someone on the other side of the portal, I couldn't be sure. I had to squint a little, as the light was so bright. The portal itself was pretty. I wondered if I could ever get my portals to look that way.

Then she stepped through. Tall, regal, calm. In the simple dark gown she'd been wearing when I saw her last. The sleeves of the gown hung down on either side of her waist. Her hands barely visible, as she clasped them across her stomach.

Oh my God. Dhysara had shown up.

Ailla reacted first. "What are you doing here?" she shrieked at Dhysara.

"I could ask you the same thing, Ailla," Dhysara said. "What are you doing here? And why are you with my husband?"

Ailla laughed. The sound had the tone of a cackle at that point. "Your husband? Dhysara, all you ever were was the smoke screen."

I'd seen Dhysara and how she thought of Cian. I knew that she was pregnant. I braced myself, waiting for her to explode. But she didn't. Dhysara looked at Ailla, and then smiled. Even to my young, inexperienced love triangle eyes, I could see that smile held lots of pity. Dhysara cradled her belly, looking down at it with a loving smile, and then looked back at Ailla.

"I was the smoke screen? Oh, no, you have that all

wrong, Ailla. I am his wife, and soon will be the mother of his child."

If ever there was a mic drop moment, this was it. Everyone in the room looked at Dhysara, but I looked at Cian. His mouth fell open and I had to say, it was nice to see how stupid he looked. For the petty side he was also the first one to find his voice again.

"You're going to have a child?" Cian asked.

Dhysara smiled, love radiating from her. "We're going to have a child, Kelan."

I'd forgotten she didn't know him as Cian.

Ailla looked at Cian, and then turned and practically flew towards Dhysara. "His name is Cian! Cian, you stupid brood mare!"

Cian grabbed Ailla by the arm as she moved by him and yanked her back down. He pulled on her so hard that she fell straight on her ass. It was glorious.

"Don't!" He barked at Ailla. For the first time since I'd met Ailla, she looked unnerved.

"Don't move," said Cian to Ailla.

I hoped she would move. I guess that made me a bad person. I took the moment to see where Brennan was. He continued to creep along the wall, inching his way closer to where Cian stood. How had he not been noticed? I didn't look the gift horse in the mouth.

Still looking at Cian, Ailla gave a little nod, but immediately turned and glared at Dhysara.

Dhysara smiled at Cian. "Thank you, my love."

"Dhysara, stay where you are. This could get dangerous."

I wondered if Dhysara could hear the completely phony tone of his voice. Watching her watching him, I didn't think so. I glanced at Taranath. The lines around his mouth were tight. He could feel the tension, too. It had been momentarily halted by the appearance of Dhysara, but the room still hummed with all the magic waiting to be called into use.

His women settled, I guess, Cian turned back to everyone else. He was completely oblivious to anything other than his own concerns. A thought hit me—he was the first truly stupid fae I'd met.

"Now, Father, it's time for you to make right has been wrong for so long."

Oh for God's sake. He was just going to make this as painful and long as possible? I knew I should be taking this seriously, but all I could think was please shut up. On that note, why didn't either of his women stab him in the eye and put us all out of our misery. I gave myself a mental shake. Focus, Iris!

"What is it you think I need to make right?" Jharak asked.

"You will step down, and proclaim me the Fae King. You will also bestow upon me the powers of the Goblin King."

I looked at Brennan, and then at Jharak. How did Cian know? I didn't think anyone knew. Wasn't the Goblin King's real job one of the big secrets of the royal family?

Cian must have seen the surprised look on everyone's faces. "You think I didn't know? Nanny Margot and Eilor told me all about it. I know exactly why you let me go, why you let me die."

Okay, he was losing it. They didn't let him die. This didn't seem the best time to interject that fact.

"I can't give you what is not mine to give," Jharak said. "The powers of the Goblin King come to the one who is chosen, and I am not one who does the choosing."

Before anyone knew what was happening, Cian darted out, grabbed Nerida, and pulled her to him. "You will do as I say, or she dies!"

"Cian!" Ailla cried, from where she still sat on the floor.

"My love, please don't do this!" Dhysara added.

Both of the women saw what Cian did not. Jharak's eyes had darkened. The energy radiating from him made me want to crawl under the table. Somehow, Cian missed all of the warning signs. He held a stone close to Nerida's face, his eyes locked on Jharak.

Perhaps he was stupid as well as crazy.

I didn't think this was going to end well.

18

Brennan

*H*e had gotten as close as he could, but when Cian grabbed Nerida, he stopped. He saw the look on Jharak's face.

He was so busy watching his parents, he didn't think to watch his wife.

Everything slowed down, and seemed to move moment by moment. Iris stepped forward around Taranath, and toward Jharak. She held out her hands, stones clutched in both and kept moving.

Brennan opened his mouth to call out to her, tell her to stop—but he was frozen with fear. Every cell cried out that he should go to her, but if he did, Cian would strike. All he could do was watch.

Two more steps brought her next to Jharak. When he realized that Iris was next to him, he held up a hand to stop her, but Iris sidestepped him and kept going.

Brennan realized too late what she was doing. He could see her mouth moving, and the look of fury on her face was something to behold. As she got closer to Cian, and the spell began to work, he could see that not only did the stones in her hands glow, but Iris herself had a glow all around her. It was almost like watching the opening of a portal. A roaring noise began, although he couldn't tell where it came from.

She was going to die. The thought rang through his head like a bell, over and over. He couldn't stop it, couldn't go to her. He looked to Drake, then Taranath —they were both still, horrified at what was playing out in front of them.

Iris reached Cian, and with one elbow, shoved Nerida out of the way. Brennan felt his heart stop. How did she manage it against Cian, when she was moving so slowly? She screamed then, something that Brennan couldn't understand, because there was a howling in the great hall that sounded like a fierce windstorm.

The tapestries on the walls flapped, and Iris shoved her glowing hands right into Cian's face. He shrieked, a horrible, inhuman sound, and dropped to the floor.

When he fell, Ailla rose, and went for—Brennan

couldn't tell if it was Iris or Cian she was aiming for. He ran for her, the frozen moment gone, meaning to intercept her, but Drake got there first. Drake caught Ailla around the waist and yanked her back.

Screaming incoherently, Ailla struck at his face.

Iris, looking up from where she stood over Cian, ran to where Drake held her and shoved her hands in Ailla's face.

The woman slid from Drake's hold into a heap on the floor.

Brennan looked away from Ailla to see Dhysara bent over, one hand to her stomach and the other to her mouth.

"What have you done?" She shrieked. "Kelan! My love!" She held out a hand to where Cian lay on the floor, tears streaming down her face.

Iris stepped around Drake, and stood in front of Dhysara. The stones were still in her hands, and she had the glow of her magic all around her. But when she spoke, she didn't even sound out of breath. "I told you if he was innocent, Dhysara, we would let him live. He was not. He would have killed everyone in this room, including you."

"No, no he wouldn't have! You murderer! You lied to me!" Dhysara wept.

"I did not. I don't lie. I have no need to. Cian—"

"Why do you call him Cian? That's not his name!" Dhysara shouted.

"It is. He was the eldest son of the Fae King, thought to have died in a fire. But he didn't die. Eilor took him in, and raised him, and let him go mad. Then he married him off to you, all while letting his daughter fall in love with that nutter as well. You're better off, Dhysara, whether you realize it or not."

When had Iris learned all this? When had she become so wise? Brennan was so proud of her that he felt as though he might burst. Let others question his choice of wife. He knew the truth. Better to focus on the good

Nerida, with the help of Jharak, finally got up. "My poor son," she said softly, looking down at Cian.

Iris whirled on her. "Your poor son? Are you kidding me? He was going to kill you, and all of us, and you're still moaning on about him? We—" she gestured to everyone in the room, "Saved your ungrateful life! And this is how you thank us? Your son died years ago. He was twisted and turned because you didn't teach him that not everything was his for the taking. And he grew up with that one's," she pointed at the lifeless Ailla, "Father. He didn't have a chance. But you knew that way back when, didn't you? You have never, ever stood up for your other sons. You know, the ones who didn't try to kill you?"

Nerida opened her mouth, but Iris cut her off.

"Unless you are going to apologize to your sons, to your husband, to all of us—you probably should be quiet." Her eyes blazed with fury.

Nerida looked to Jharak, who looked back at her without saying anything. She looked around the room. No one knew what to say, Brennan could tell. He understood. It wasn't often that one witnessed the queen of the Fae being given what for.

Iris broke the awkward silence. She rushed to him, wrapping her arms around him. "What are you doing out of bed? You're not ready for this!"

He cradled her to him, realizing how much he'd missed her. "I woke to find you gone. I knew something was wrong. I couldn't stay away. You know that. How could you take such a chance?" The thought that he could have lost her—he couldn't speak.

"I know I'm nagging," she said into his shoulder. "But I have to say it anyway. And what do you mean, how could I take the chance? I love you." He could feel a dampness and knew that she was crying.

A shout made him thrust Iris behind him.

Cian had risen, and the look of madness on him— Brennan felt a fear for those he couldn't protect. He lifted his sword. He might die, but he would kill Cian before he did.

A burst of light hit Cian in the midsection, and he

fell once more. Brennan searched for the source—and saw Taranath, arms outstretched.

Drake, who had hit the ground when someone—Brennan didn't know who— shouted, got up and nudged at Cian. He looked around, meeting Brennan's eyes. "He's gone."

Nerida slid against Jharak, onto the floor. She covered her face with her hands. Brennan had to avert his eyes. While harsh, everything Iris had said was true. It was difficult to look at his mother with anything other than anger for the moment.

He realized that Cian was very like her. Determined to see what they wanted to see until the end.

Another flash of light burst out, this time going towards Drake. A small, dark figure hit Drake, knocking him to the floor.

"Damn you, Aine! What are you doing?" screamed Ailla. She had sat up, and her outstretched hand told Brennan that she'd tried to kill Drake.

Before Ailla could say anything else, she was hit in the midsection with a spell.

Who had cast it? Brennan looked at everyone else in the room before he saw Dhysara with a stone in her hand.

"You are going to—" Ailla stopped in the middle of her words, and the most extraordinary expression came over her face. "What?" she asked softly, and then fell to the floor.

Brennan felt fairly sure that this time, she, like Cian was no more.

Dhysara walked over, staring down at Ailla. "He was mine. You always did want everything for yourself. But he was mine. Even to the end." Then she stepped over Ailla as though she were nothing, and went to Cian.

She knelt down, caressing his cheek. "My love. We could have been happy. But you let them turn you." She bent over, and kissed him tenderly.

Nerida audibly sobbed. Brennan couldn't look at her.

Dhysara rose. She walked to Taranath. He crossed his arms, looking wary as she approached.

"Mage, can you make me forget?"

"I beg your pardon, my lady?"

"Can you make me forget? I do not wish to remember any of this. Take it away. I want to only remember Kelan, and the life I thought we had." Her voice, although low, rang out through the hall.

"Are you sure, my lady?" Taranath asked respectfully.

She nodded. "I am. This is nothing I want to remember. I would like to raise my child in peace, and in health."

Nerida spoke then. "That is our—" She stopped as Jharak cut her off.

"We would be happy to help you."

"Thank you, your Majesty. As I told your daughter-in-law, I no longer wish to concern myself with the quarrels of the past. I only want to look to the future."

Jharak nodded to Taranath. "Would you take the Lady Dhysara with you, and prepare her for what she asks? I shall join you shortly."

Taranath offered Dhysara his arm, which she took. She did not look at anyone, not even Cian, as she walked to the door of the hall, and then out.

There was a moment of silence, and then Nerida burst out, "That is our grandchild, Jharak! She can't—"

Brennan stepped forward then. "He can, and he will, Mother. It is time for this to end. You will need to manage your mourning in private, and you will never speak of this again."

Nerida drew herself up. "How dare you speak to me! I am the—"

"I dare." Jharak said.

Nerida stopped. Brennan could see that she hadn't expected to hear from her husband.

"It is over, Nerida. Our son, as Iris so correctly pointed out, died many years ago. The man that stood here today was not our son. He was the creature of the Dragon King, and whatever plans were made in that

Realm. That is a child of the man would have killed you, killed us all. We do not want or need such a child in our midst. We have enough to settle and deal with. I would suggest," he added, seeing her begin to speak again, "That you exercise prudence, and take your leave. I will join you later," and he turned towards Brennan and Drake.

Brennan felt sorry for his mother, but she had made this choice. She'd made the choice years ago, but only now did it come to fruition.

Wordlessly, Nerida left the hall.

"You're going to pay for that," Drake said to Jharak.

A smile creased his father's face. "I always do. But she will come round."

"I hope you're right, Father," Brennan said.

"Are you all right?" Jharak leaned down and helped Aine up. "I owe you my thanks for saving my son."

Aine seemed uncomfortable with the praise. "She'd hurt so many people. I knew..." she glanced at Drake. "I knew who you were. She'd talked about you. You didn't deserve to die like that."

Drake looked away, his cheeks flushing.

Jharak stepped in. "Whatever your reasons, I thank you. Now, let us get all of this taken care of after we see to ourselves and our hurts." He waved at the hall, which lay in ruins.

Brennan hadn't realized that tables and chairs and

the tapestries on the walls had been tossed about and torn off. When did that happen?

Jharak looked around, and not, Brennan noticed, at the bodies on the ground. "Shall we?" He offered his arm to Aine. "Drake, would you come with me?"

The three of them walked out of the hall, and Brennan could hear his father speaking to Aine.

He looked at Iris, and she ran to him.

"Finally," she said.

"Oh?"

"I didn't get much of a honeymoon," she added.

He laughed. "So I hear. Trolls and a dungeon?"

"Not even what I wanted to do. Do you know how much they smell?"

He laughed again as he led her away. As they left the hall, he closed the door. They would remove the bodies discreetly, and no one would ever know.

As Dhysara said, it was time to look to the future.

Iris

*a*fter the scene in the great hall, I felt like I was going to fall asleep standing up, but the thought of being with Brennan kept me going. We walked towards our rooms, not speaking, holding hands. I think he had the same idea that I did.

Thinking about the dream I'd had of him when we were looking for him made my pulse quicken. He'd been too tired and worn last night for me to do anything other than wrap myself around him and fall asleep, content that he was finally back with me, where he belonged.

But now? With the light of battle in our eyes, so to speak? And him obviously feeling better? Oh, it was time for the sexy times. For real. No dreams.

He wrenched open the door, and pulled me in after him. Before the door was closed, he had grabbed me, and pushed me against the wall, kissing me fiercely. I ran my fingers through his hair, loving the feel of him.

I'd missed his touch for so long, wanted to touch him every day. Not knowing if he was alive or dead— and now, here he was. Real, in the flesh, and...oh, just as ready as I was.

I wrapped my legs around him as he turned, moving towards the bed. I could have gotten things going right at the door, but after what seemed like sleeping on the ground forever, a bed sounded good.

His knees bumped the edge of the bed, and I unwound my legs to kneel on the bed in front of him. I took off my top, and then his.

"When did you bring your human clothes?" he murmured into my mouth.

"When we had to go and find your ass," I said.

He laughed against my face, and I could feel the thrill of desire shoot all the way to below the waistline. Speaking of which, Brennan's hands went to my buttons, and expertly, for a guy who didn't deal with them, he undid them, and slid the jeans down my legs. I stood up, and let him slide them off, one leg at a time.

"What is this, my lady? Nothing under your clothing?"

I giggled. I'd forgotten to pack underwear in my mad dash home.

"The better to greet you with, don't you think?"

He leaned against me then, his head next to my stomach. "To feel your skin next to mine, to smell you, my beloved...I wasn't sure I'd see you again."

I reached down, and took his face in my hands. "I would never let you go, Brennan. Never. Would you have left me to die?"

"Never."

"That goes both ways, pal. And why are you still dressed?"

He slid off his trousers, and melded his body next to mine as we fell onto the bed. He was still too thin, but his body was warm and felt so good next to me.

"I don't know if I can wait," he breathed into my neck. "I've seen you in my dreams so many times, that I can't stand to wait."

"Don't."

That one word energized him. He pulled me to him, and into the middle of the bed. He kissed my neck, nipping gently at my collarbone. Then he bent his head and took my nipple into his mouth, sucking hard. I arched towards him. I didn't know if I could wait either.

Brennan slid an arm under me, pulling me closer. He bit down on my other nipple, and I felt the rush of wetness between my legs. This was so much better than a dream.

"I need you," he murmured.

"Take me," I replied.

We didn't go to sleep for a long time.

19

Iris

I stretched, feeling sore in all sorts of right places. We'd made love twice more before finally falling asleep in one another's arms. My arm fell to the other side of the bed and found it empty. I sat up, heart racing.

Brennan stood by the window, trousers on, but with no shirt. I admired the muscles of his back. Even thin, he was still the most handsome, sexy, attractive man I'd ever seen. I took the sheet from the bed, wrapping it around me as I swung my legs out, and walked over to him. I wrapped my arms around him, laying my head on his back.

"Are you all right?"

"I was thinking what a waste this all was, what a mess."

"This is not your fault, Brennan."

"You could have died, Iris."

I slid under his arm so I could see him. "You could have died, Brennan."

He opened his mouth, and then closed it. "Yes, and I nearly did. Had Aine not come in and healed me, I would have."

"Who is she?" I asked.

"I am not sure. She was some part of Eilor's schemes. That much I know. We thought it was all Cian, but from what Cian, Ailla, and Aine have said, this was the doing of Eilor."

I thought about the Dragon King. From what I'd seen, he didn't put out the crafty schemer vibe. I said so.

"No, he did not. Which makes him all the more dangerous. We have to find him."

"What will happen to Dhysara?"

He looked out the window, shrugging lightly. "I'm not sure. I have some ideas, but it will depend on Father."

"I'm sorry about your mom," I said. I could have kicked her ass, but no one wanted to see their mom like that.

Brennan sighed. "It will take time, but she will

heal. I'm not sure she'll get over the loss of a grandchild soon, however. That may take a while longer."

I ducked my head into his chest, smiling to myself. "Well, maybe not."

Silence. Then he pushed me away from him, holding my arms.

"What are you saying, Iris?"

This was not quite the reception I'd been expecting. But I couldn't stop from smiling as I said, "Well, she's about to get a grandchild from the non-crazy side of the family."

"You're sure?"

Shit. I couldn't tell what he was thinking.

"I am."

"That was...that was very fast." His brow furrowed.

"We had a lot of sex before you were kidnapped."

"No, no...just that fae women—"

"Mostly human, remember?" I pointed at myself. "No matter what else may be changing. We get pregnant pretty quickly when you're not using any birth control."

"What?"

"Nothing. Listen, genius, I'm getting a little upset here. Are you happy about this or not? Or do you need to interrogate me some more?"

His face went completely blank, and then he

picked me up off the ground and crushed me to him. "Am I happy? Of course, I am happy! I didn't expect that we'd be parents so soon."

He kissed me, the big smile that was on my face blooming on his.

"Why don't we go back to bed?" I asked, letting the sheet fall as much as I could while he held me.

"But we're—"

"Later. Bed!" I pointed behind him.

We were late for breakfast that morning.

Brennan

*H*and in hand, he walked with Iris towards the smaller dining room. His father had sent a servant asking that they join him for a late mid-afternoon meal. Brennan smiled. He understood that Jharak was needling him a bit about not being up earlier, but he felt that he had earned a late morning with his wife.

He'd asked Iris if he could share their news, and she'd agreed. He was so excited he didn't know what to do with himself. An heir had always been an expected thing, but he hadn't seen himself in the role as a father. The role of a husband was so new...but to know that he would be a father and a father to Iris' child...he looked down at the top of her head, and kissed it.

She smiled up at him, and he could see the roses in her cheeks. Already she looked even more beautiful.

He couldn't wait to share the news. They reached the door of the dining room, and he pushed it open to come upon Jharak and Drake, nose to nose, arguing.

"I won't do it!" Drake said, almost shouting.

"You must. There is no one else that I trust." Jharak was calm.

"Are we interrupting?" he asked politely.

Drake turned to him, furious. "Tell him! Tell him, Bren! Tell him I cannot be a king!"

"Why not? You're the son of a king."

Drake looked at him. Whatever he'd been expecting, this wasn't it. "Thank you, brother. Good to know you've got my back in a fight." Then he turned back to Jharak. "The Dragon Realm already has a king."

"A traitor, who even now has disappeared. You heard what Aine told us this morning. The court was in chaos even before Cian made his move. We cannot leave things the way they are. Someone completely unsuitable will rise to power. We cannot have anyone other than one of ours in power. Not with that court. Not with the dragons."

"Then let her do it!" Drake gestured to Aine.

She shook her head. "I've told you. The court knows me as some sort of experiment. They would never trust me. I am too closely tied to Eilor in their minds. And I don't want to rule. I do want to go back, because I want to make sure the dragons are cared for."

"Why don't we just kill them, and the threat will be done?" Brennan asked.

Aine stood, and Brennan took a step back at the ferocity in her face. "Why don't I kill you, because you come from the wrong stock? They have done nothing for centuries, other than what Eilor forced them too! I'm not demanding we go and kill your ancestors, am I? I don't know exactly how I am part of it, but I am part of the dragons. They will be protected, or I will not help you!"

Jharak held up a hand. "The dragons are not going to be harmed. I've been speaking with Aine for some time. Most of the dragons are sleeping, spelled into a dream state. Am I correct?"

She nodded, some of the ferocity fading from her. "As best I can tell. He was very secretive about what he did with them."

"Where do you think he is?" Brennan asked.

"I've sent Taranath and a contingent of guards to the Dragon Realm. I hope you don't mind—" Jharak spoke to Brennan. "I felt he was the wisest choice. The fewer people who know the truth, the better."

Brennan nodded. "What's been done with Cian and Ailla?"

"We disposed of them this morning. Buried in unmarked areas, far from here." Drake sounded almost normal.

"Did you tell Mother?"

Jharak shook his head. "No. I felt it best that I take care of this on my own."

"I don't envy you that conversation. Where did you send Dhysara?"

"We have not sent her anywhere yet. She's been keeping to her rooms. When he returns, I will have Taranath remove her memories. But I wanted to speak with you about this, Brennan. Where should we locate her? While she's said nothing—I don't think she should be in the same place she was before." Jharak looked concerned.

Iris spoke then. "Can Taranath actually reorder her memories?"

Brennan answered her. "Yes, he can. We would never do this without someone requesting it. It's very rare that they do. But I don't feel her request is out of order."

Iris squeezed his hand, and he felt a thrill of desire shoot through him. Something about the thought of her carrying his child made it hard for him to concentrate.

She let go and went to sit down next to Aine at the table. Brennan could tell, although they had not spoken of it, that Iris liked the other woman. Given how jealous she'd been before, he was glad to see it. He knew, in his mind, that the jealousy was part of the spell Ailla had put on Iris; that didn't mean he wasn't aware of the possibility.

One more reason to be glad that Ailla was gone.

"What are you going to tell everyone about Ailla?" Iris asked. "Won't the Dragon Court be upset? What will Eilor think?"

"He is probably gone," Aine said. She spoke quietly, but everyone turned to her. "He was not entirely for kidnapping you, but Cian wouldn't listen to anyone other than himself, and Ailla long ago aligned herself with Cian."

"Gone?" Drake asked. "Where would he go?"

Aine shrugged. "I don't know. I just know that he would disappear at times for days on end, and he didn't even tell Ailla where he'd been."

"We have to assume he's alive, and in hiding. All more reason for you to—" Jharak said to Drake.

Drake's easy humor vanished. "No! I don't want it!" He glared around the room, and stomped over towards the window, kicking one of the chairs at the table as he did so.

Aine, who had ignored Drake's outburst in favor

of the fruit plate in front of her, looked up. "You need to. Someone does. The Realm will go to pieces otherwise." She took a bite of fruit and spoke through her chewing. "I'll help you. I can't rule, but I know the court. I can help you, or whomever it is that goes, to sort things out." She focused on the plate again.

"There," Jharak said. "You have an insider who will help you. There's no one else I can trust, Drake."

At the window, hands clenched on the stone sill, Drake's shoulders tensed. Brennan understood. It was hard to resist their father when he was asking for help. He so rarely did so.

The room fell silent, everyone waiting to see what Drake would say. Brennan walked towards his brother and put a hand on his shoulder. "Brother, you are suited for this. I know you don't want it, but you are. You have been my rock for years. It's time to be your own rock."

He knew Drake didn't want this, but he also knew this was the right thing. He could feel it. Even as he didn't want to lose his best friend, Drake needed to find his place that was his, and his alone. Not as a part of the life of another.

"Leave you to your wife? Hope she doesn't brain you in your sleep?" Drake asked, staring down at the sill. "You won't make it a year, brother."

"Well then I'll have the Goblin Realm all to myself," Iris said from the table. "Not a bad deal."

A moment, and then everyone, even Drake, laughed. Brennan shot a glance of gratitude towards Iris, and he could see that Aine smiled. That was a good sign as well. He hadn't seen a smile from her since he'd met her that wasn't tinged with bitterness or sarcasm.

This was genuine, and it gave him hope for Drake and what he could accomplish.

"All right, all right!" Drake hit the sill. "I'll go. I am making no promises, none at all!" He turned to glare at both Jharak and Brennan. "I will go, and see what kind of mess that family of lunatics has left, and only then will I decide whether I stay."

When neither Jharak nor Brennan responded, he continued, "And that's it! That is the only promise you will get from me. If you're going to yoke me to a throne, then I will determine whether or not it's worth it." His gaze landed on Aine. "And you will help me in whatever I need. I'm not going into that nest of vipers blind!"

She nodded, not even looking up from the fruit. "Of course. I want to see the Realm regain its health. I will be happy to help you."

Drake threw up his hands, and stomped towards the door. He jerked it open, saying, "I need to go. I've lost my appetite!" The door slammed behind him as he left.

"Well, that went super well," Iris said.

"He'll come round," Jharak didn't sound concerned as he sat down at the table. "He knows it's the best way for all of us. I appreciate your willingness to help him, my dear," he said to Aine, smiling.

She met his eyes. "I have no choice, either. If I do not, the dragons will be killed. If not by you, then by the people of the Dragon Realm."

"How do you know?" Iris asked.

"Eilor used them as a way to inspire fear. No one knows much about them, only that he has some kept locked away. People probably think more than there are, but that's what fear does, right?"

"I'm glad you'll be with him," Iris said.

Aine looked up at that.

"Really?"

20

Iris

I smiled at her. "Yes, I will. I'm sad, though, because I would have liked to have you here longer." I hoped she could tell that my words were genuine.

Aine returned the smile, and it pleased me. I noticed she didn't smile often. It made me kind of sad to think why that was—that she'd not had a lot of reason to smile.

"He needs the help," was all she said.

But I could tell that my words pleased her as well. The sense that this would be a friend that I'd had from the beginning increased.

I turned my mind to another matter. "That doesn't

help you, though, does it?" I asked Jharak.

He frowned slightly. "What do you mean? And Brennan, please sit down. It disturbs the ability to eat in peace with you looming."

I looked down to hide my smile. It was funny to see how Brennan's parents—well, his dad—talked to him sometimes.

Brennan sat, and I continued. "You still don't have an heir to the Fae Throne."

One blond eyebrow arched at my words. "Are you predicting my demise sometime soon, Iris? Letting me know that I should get my affairs in order?"

I laughed. "No, don't be silly. But this whole mess involved who gets to be king, right? If Drake is the Dragon King, then who takes over thousands of years from now for you? Do you have, like, a cousin or something?" I looked around the table.

Jharak smiled. "I have found that these things have a way of working themselves out. I've been concerned over Eilor's reign for some time, but hadn't seen a solution to it. Now one has presented itself, and while it will take time, it will be the correct solution."

"I'll enjoy watching you make that happen," Brennan said to his father, the dry tone showing his humor.

Jharak waved a hand at Brennan. "You'll see. It will work out as it's supposed to."

I decided to take the bull by the horns. "Where's Nerida?" I asked.

"She's keeping to our rooms. She's not happy with any of us at the moment," Jharak said.

"Oh? Will that all work out, too?" Brennan teased.

I was relieved to see that Brennan didn't seem too put out by his mother's behavior, or sulking. I supposed that it was because she'd seen her child die... but I found that I couldn't feel a lot of sympathy. The guy was nuts. He'd have murdered us all if he could have. He had to die so that we could live.

But I guess she didn't see it that way. I mentally shrugged to myself. That was going to be her problem to manage.

Talk turned to other, lighter subjects, and we'd all finished eating when a member of the household staff burst in, red-faced and flustered.

"Your Majesty, I am sorry—" he began, but he was shoved out of the way by someone coming through the door.

Jharak and Brennan were on their feet instantly.

I had stood also, and backed closer to the wall. Then I peered at the person who burst in.

"Mara?"

I couldn't believe it. My grandmother, in her human clothing, stood next to the poor staff guy, hands on hips, and she was pissed.

"Well, so you're safe." Her anger landed on me.

"Uh...why wouldn't I be?"

"Claire and Paul called me, and told me that you and that brother of yours," she directed this at Brennan, "Had shown up and grabbed a bunch of things and been shifty as hell! What is going on? And don't lie to me, especially you!" She glared at Jharak.

"Imara, how nice to see you again. It's been a long time. Please sit down," Jharak gestured towards the table. "Can we offer you some refreshment?"

"Don't pull the pleasantries with me, Jharak. You haven't exactly been on my good list. Not then, and not now. Neither you nor Nerida."

What was that about? That suggested a lot more than she or Nerida had mentioned. I made a mental note to ask when she wasn't ready to tear someone's hair out.

"Mara, how did you get here?" I asked. "I'm fine, by the way. Things went sideways, but they're better now. And I'm glad you're here." I walked over to her, giving her a hug. I found that I was glad—we could share our news, and then my mom and dad would know soon.

She held my face in her hands. "You're really all right? I know the scheming of this family. You're not lying to me?"

"I don't lie. You know that."

She hugged me back. "It's good to see you again,

my girl." She stood back, hands on my shoulders. "Something is different, though. What is it?" She peered at me.

I couldn't stop the smile. I glanced at Brennan, and then to everyone else. "Well, it looks like you're going to be a great-granny."

She stared, and then a grin spread across her face. "Really? You're sure?"

I nodded, feeling the tears prick at the corner of my eyes.

She pulled me to her, hugging me tightly.

The impact of what I'd said hit Jharak, and he was hugging Brennan. Even Aine offered congratulations, her eyes showing that she was pleased for us.

Mara sat next to me as I began to share the story of how we'd found Brennan.

"Oh, shit!" I exclaimed as a thought came to me.

"What?" several voices asked at once.

"We need to go pay a visit to some wolves," I grinned, thinking about it.

This was going to be fun.

Maybe Jharak was right. Things did have a way of working out.

———

The End

*H*ere ends (begins?) the story of Brennan & Iris.

But the Realm has expanded and grown in a way I hadn't expected.

So look for Book 4 in The Realm series, RISE OF THE DRAGON KING. This story developed because it had to happen. Book 4 will follow Drake, Brennan's right hand guy – as he steps out on his own.

And this is because of you, my readers, asking me, "So what happens to Drake? You realize you broke his heart, right?"

I heard you. Book 4 will be out by the summer of 2017.

There are also going to be a number of short stories that deal with happenings in the Realm. Follow me on Amazon to keep up with them – they will all be labeled as A Realm Companion Story. After the last Realm Companion Story (Eilor's Tale), a new series, The Dragon Thief, will begin. I'm so excited to share all of these stories with you all! Thank you for being part of this!

Keep up with me via my Newsletter (where you'll also get first looks, sneak peeks, and special offers just for my readers!) or on Amazon so you don't miss any releases!

ACKNOWLEDGMENTS

No book, no author, is an island. Well, we are, but we are on the island, waving at the support planes that buzz overhead. This is my attempt to thank all the people who drop care packages on me regularly.

First, to my two favorite writerly types: Rachel Millar, who does my editing. She is not, however, the last pair of grubby mitts that touches the story – so all mistakes are mine. I'm sorry, Rachel, if I messed up your good works. I try! Thank you for all that you have done to make the Realm become a reality. Here we are, Book 3, and it's still...not...done!

Then, thank you to Corinne O'Flynn. Another ear to bounce ideas off of is worth its weight in gold. And so, so much more.

My accountability partner, Wendy Howard. I love

knowing that I have to keep moving forward. Except when the plague strikes. Then I allow for a pass on the updates!

My children, who are my biggest fans. Their shining support is beyond amazing. My husband, who makes this possible. I love you all. I'm so fortunate that it's the three of you sharing my life.

To Judy Crane, Linden Price, and Shannon Scanlon – your unwavering belief. I love that the most recent thing I heard from my family was, "I can't keep up with all your new releases!" You all have never doubted me, not even for a minute.

To my amazing writers' organization, Rocky Mountain Fiction Writers. If I hadn't found this group, I would still be flailing in the wilderness, wondering what to do. Knowing that you have a tribe, and where to find them is the best thing about being an author. That there are other people who *get it.* Thank you.

Finally, thank you to my readers. Brennan and Iris have been hanging around like bats in the belfry for a while. But thanks to you all, I have teased them out, and given them a happy ending, as ALL stories should be.

Lisa Manifold,
March 2017

ALSO BY LISA MANIFOLD

The Sisters of the Curse Series

Thea's Tale

One Night at the Ball

Casimir's Journey

Heart of the Djinn Series

Three Wishes

Forgotten Wishes (2017)

Hidden Wishes (2017)

The Realm Series

Heart of the Goblin King

To Wed the Goblin King

Realms of the Goblin King

Rise of the Dragon King

The Realm Companion Stories, Vol. 1 (2017)

The Realm Companion Stories, Vol. 2 (2017)

continued...

ABOUT LISA MANIFOLD

Lisa Manifold is a USA Today Bestselling Author of fantasy, paranormal, and romance stories. She moved to Colorado as an adult and has no plans of living anywhere else. She is a consummate reader, often running late because "Just one more page!" She is a fan of all things Con, and has an entire room devoted to the costumes created for Cons. She serves on the board of Rocky Mountain Fiction Writers as the Independent Published Author Liaison, and in 2016, was named the RMFW Independent Writer of the Year.

Lisa is the author of the fae paranormal romance series The Realm, the Grimm fairy tale retelling Sisters of the Curse series, the Heart of the Djinn series which follows a free-lance djinn, the Aumahnee Prophecy urban fantasy series, and the forthcoming urban fantasy series The Dragon Thief.

She lives as close to the mountains as possible with her husband, sons, and two attentive dogs.

You can stay in touch! Just head over to Lisa's website, where you can sign up for her Newsletter to keep up with all the news and members-only offers.

Stay connected...
www.lisamanifold.com